HIS TO LOVE

AN ARRANGED MARRIAGE ROMANCE (IRRESISTIBLE BROTHERS 5)

SCARLETT KING

MICHELLE LOVE

CONTENTS

Blurb	1
1. Patton	3
2. Alexa	10
3. Patton	17
4. Alexa	23
5. Patton	30
6. Alexa	37
7. Patton	44
8. Alexa	50
9. Patton	57
10. Alexa	65
11. Patton	70
12. Alexa	76
13. Patton	84
14. Alexa	91
15. Patton	98
16. Alexa	104
17. Patton	111
18. Alexa	117
19. Patton	123
20. Alexa	130
21. Patton	137
22. Alexa	144
23. Patton	150
24. Alexa	157
25. Patton	164
26. Alexa	172
27. Patton	179
28. Alexa	187
Epilogue	196

Made in "The United States" by:

Scarlett King & Michelle Love

© Copyright 2021

ISBN: 978-1-64808-775-2

ALL RIGHTS RESERVED. No part of this publication may be reproduced or transmitted in any form whatsoever, electronic, or mechanical, including photocopying, recording, or by any informational storage or retrieval system without express written, dated and signed permission from the author

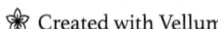 Created with Vellum

BLURB

I've never been one to ignore a friend in need. And he's my best friend.
His family has been good to me my whole life.
How can I turn him down when he and his family need me the most?
I've known her for her whole life. She's the younger sister of my best friend. The little angel of her family.
I know she's just about as precious as her family thinks she is. But perfection never lasts, and she made a decision that would change her life— *and mine.*
There has always been platonic love between us.
Will marriage—even a fake one—transform that love into something more?
Could her brother ever give us his blessing if we blossom into more?
I have my doubts. I have my worries.
But I can't let my fears get in the way of making her mine—for real.
I can't let anyone get in the way of what just might be true love.

We will become a real family. I can't let it be any other way.

1

PATTON

"Alejandra De La Cruz is here to see you, Mr. Nash."

Alexa. It had been a few years since I'd seen my best friend's little sister. "Send her in, Callie."

Back in Houston, Luciano De La Cruz and I had been lifelong friends since kindergarten. His family had always been exceptionally good to me after my parents were killed in a house fire when I was just sixteen.

When I told him that the resort and spa my brothers and I had just opened in Austin was hiring, he asked me if I could interview his sister for a massage therapist position. She'd just finished studies at her vocational training school to become one, and was looking to get her foot in the door. It was my honor to hire his sister after all his parents had done for me.

But he wanted me to formally interview her anyway. Luciano knew she needed to feel confident that she earned the job on her own, not just because she was Luci's baby sister. So, I played along.

Meeting her at my office door, I opened my arms. "Alexa, I'm so glad to see you."

Shyly, she ducked her head as she moved into my embrace.

"Patton, I'm so happy you're giving me the chance to interview to work at your beautiful resort."

I let her go and turned to lead her into my office. "Take a seat, Miss De La Cruz." I wanted to give her the full interview experience. "I've read your resume and must point out that you have no on-the-job experience. Can you tell me how much training you've had with actual clients?" I took my seat behind the desk, steepling my fingers as I awaited her response.

She held herself with poise, her posture perfect, hands placed neatly in her lap. She looked every bit the professional we were looking for. "Mr. Nash," she played along with me without having to be prompted, "my training at the Academy of Therapeutic Message was extensive. While learning about the various muscles and the way to properly manipulate them, I also received daily hands-on training. The program was eighteen months long, and the number of massages I have given is well over two hundred."

"Over two hundred?" I found that impressive.

Her attire was also on point for the position she was after. Her long, dark hair was pulled back into a nice and neat ponytail. She wore a white button-down shirt tucked into a pair of black slacks, and black flats.

"Yes, Mr. Nash, over two hundred. I have perfected my technique for visceral massage, which focuses on the abdomen. It is a very helpful massage for people who experience back pain, have had internal injuries, and even those who suffer from constipation."

"Sounds like great therapy." I could already see that she'd be a great part of the team we were building at Whispers Resort and Spa. But there was one major concern.

"Alexa, I did read your resume, so I know you've got what it takes to become a member of the staff here. The therapies and techniques you've trained in sound like they're exactly what we're looking for. My concerns lie in how your parents will take you moving to Austin from your home in Houston. I know how protective they are. And, may I ask, what is the plan for your accommodations if you have to relocate?"

I could see her squirming as she pressed her lips into a thin line, but only for a moment before she looked into my eyes. "My parents have made arrangements for me to live with a deacon from the local church if I am employed by you, Mr. Nash. Deacon Soliz and his wife have agreed to allow me to stay with them, as their son has been gone for the last few years. He's attending UCLA, so he moved to California. They say they'll be happy to have someone around the house again now that he's gone."

Alexa had been sent to a private Catholic school as a girl, while Luciano had been allowed to go to public school. Her parents always spared nothing to keep her out of harm's way. It was a little hard for me to believe that they would actually be on board with her moving so far from home.

"Alexa, let's talk as old friends for a moment. I know the sheltered life you've lived for twenty-two years." Luci and I had been ten when she was born. She was what Mrs. De La Cruz called her little miracle— and Alexa had always been treated as such. "Are your parents behind you working and living two and a half hours away from them?"

"Patton," she said, her dark eyes shining, her full lips curving into a smile, "I would not be here if they were not behind me on this. They trust you—you know that. And they trust the Soliz family. They believe I am in good hands."

And she would be—with me at least. Her naivety was something that worried me though. She'd lived with her parents even after graduating high school. She'd gone to community college after that for a couple of years before going to the vocational school. All the while she'd lived at home with her parents.

Moving to Austin, living on her own—this would be such a huge change for her. I wasn't sure she was ready for the real world. "If you have any concerns about the people you'll be staying with, you *will* come to me, right?" I wanted her to know that I would always be there for her, no matter what. "Your brother is my best friend. I won't let anything happen to you. But I want to be sure that you're ready for all the changes that will happen if you get this job."

"I want to gain some freedom from my parents, Patton. I love them dearly, but they've held me back from so many things. I mean, I had to take my cousin Baldo to prom because they didn't trust anyone else to take me." I could hear the exasperation in her voice, but she looked shyly down at the floor while she spoke, her hands wringing in her lap.

"I've been kept away from the world in many ways. Never allowed to date." She looked at me with pleading eyes. "I'm twenty-two and I've never been allowed to go out on a date. Not that I've been asked." She blushed a little at that. That she'd never been asked out came as a shock to me. Her shyness must put men off—there was certainly nothing wrong with her looks. Or anything else about her.

I shook off my thoughts as she continued. "But I want to shed that skin and grow a new one. And I can't do that with my loving parents hovering over me all the time."

She was right, they did hover. But how would she cope with this sudden freedom? I had to make sure she knew that I would be there for her. "Alexa, as long as you understand that you can come to me with anything, any problem, any worry, anything at all, then I think this might be a great opportunity for you. But independence isn't all it's cracked up to be. There will be bills to pay, and you will be responsible for yourself out here."

Nodding, she seemed as if she'd been thinking about that. "I've got my own car that I would like to start making the payments on, so my father doesn't have to any longer. He's given me so much in my life, and I'd like to be able to take the financial burden off his shoulders. And I'd like to take the stress off my mother as well. I know she feels entirely responsible for my well-being. Has Luciano told you of her heart condition?"

He had not. "No." I frowned. Strange, that he would keep something so serious from me.

"Perhaps he didn't want to worry you, since you've been so busy with building this place and getting it up and running. He said you oversaw the interior design." She looked around my office in approval. "And may I say that you've done an amazing job. This place is beautiful."

No matter how busy I'd been, I would've wanted my best friend to know that I had time for him to lean on me over his mother's health. "How is she, Alexa?"

"She has good days and bad ones." Her eyes shimmered a bit as she looked up, trying not to let her emotions get the best of her. "She began feeling light-headed, and at times there was pain in her chest. Dad took her to the doctor and they found that her heart fluttered at times. They said she's got an arrhythmia and that she has to be careful because it can cause blood clots. Times of stress are especially hard on her."

"And you're not worried that your moving away will upset her?" I thought it would most certainly upset her.

"I think it will make her feel better to know that I can take care of myself. I think that will bring her some comfort, Patton."

"Maybe you're right. But if she begins to get worse, then you'd need to go to her, right?" I was sure Alexa would leave the job behind if her mother needed her. "Not that I'd be against hiring you if that's the case. I'm just asking as a friend."

Nodding, she seemed to understand. "I would go to her. But I'm not sure if I would stay—not unless my presence made a difference in her condition. I've done everything they've asked of me. I've lived life on their terms. It's time I got to live life on *my* terms."

It seemed she'd been thinking a lot about how to get out from under her parents' wings. It made me wonder just when exactly she'd started taking a more active role in her decisions. "Alexa, did you want to go to school for massage therapy, or was that something your parents wanted?"

"I see why you're asking me that question. You're afraid this isn't my passion, but theirs." Taking a deep breath, she went on. "I was the one who looked into the idea. Of course, me being me, I went to my parents to see what they thought about it before I made up my mind. To be honest, my father didn't approve of it at first. He thought I would end up working in some sleazy place where men would expect certain things from me."

"We don't allow that sort of thing here," I let her know. "We have a strict code of conduct for our employees. In the contract, you'll see that we have a clause forbidding any sexual relationships between employees and clients. It would be grounds for immediate dismissal if we catch a member of our staff in a compromising position with any client—and that's within this resort and outside of it as well."

Knowing I'd be offering her the position, I figured I might as well fill her in on our more of our expectations. "We don't allow tips here either. You will be paid well. There's no need for our customers to give you anything on their own. No tickets to sporting events or passes to nightclubs, nothing. We expect you to politely refuse their offers while not offending them in any way. Our guests will be made aware of our rules, so they shouldn't offer you anything anyway."

"I understand." Her lips quirked to one side. "It sort of sounds like you're telling me that I *will* be working here."

She'd had the job before I ever spoke a word to her. But I

didn't want her to know that. "I think this interview went very well. How do you feel about it?"

"I think it went well too. I know I can be an asset to Whispers Resort and Spa. You can always depend on me to be professional, both with our guests and the other staff members. I will read every rule you have and will follow them all."

I knew she knew how to obey without questioning anything. She'd never done so much as talk back to her parents. She'd been the most obedient child I'd ever known. And sweet, too. Alexa was a little angel, just like her parents often called her. Her brother called her *princesa*.

I stood and walked around my desk, holding out my hand to her. She took it and I shook it. "Welcome aboard, Alejandra Consuela Christina De La Cruz, it's a pleasure to have you on our team."

Her grin went from ear to ear, the happiness radiating on her face. "You will not be disappointed with my work, Mr. Nash."

2
ALEXA

"Mom, I got the job!" I was full of excitement as I drove to my new home.

"Congratulations, I knew you could do it," she gushed. "How is our friend Patton doing?"

"He seems fine. He sends his regards and he told me to let you and Daddy know that he'll watch over me for you guys." I shivered as adrenaline rushed through me. "Ahh! I can't believe it! I got a job—the job of my dreams!"

"I am so proud of you. Your father will be too. I'll let him know the good news as soon as he gets home from work. Are you going to the deacon's home now, Alejandra?"

"I am. Should you give him a call first?" I wasn't sure how I would be able to do that, as my father had made all the arrangements with Deacon Soliz.

I heard the sound of papers rustling before she said, "I found the note your father left me. It says to punch in nine-six-nine-seven on the keypad to get into the house. You've got the address, right?"

"I do." I was surprised how easy everything was going. I was so afraid I would feel out of sorts with so many changes happening at once, but all I felt was excitement and happiness.

"The note also says that both the deacon and his wife work and don't get home until six each night. So, you'll be alone in the house for a while. Are you okay with that? If not, I'm sure Patton will let you hang around at the resort until then."

"I'd actually like a little time at the house by myself anyway. That'll give me a chance to unpack my things so that when they do come home, I can spend some time with them and get to know them a bit." Feeling incredibly optimistic about the job interview, I'd brought all of the basics I'd need for my new life with me.

I knew it would be odd to live with people I'd never met before, but it was worth it to finally have the chance to be on my own. Plus, I could always hang out with Patton if I felt too uncomfortable.

Patton and my brother had been friends forever. He'd been at our home almost every day as I grew up. I felt at ease with him and always had. He was a familiar face in a sea of unfamiliarity.

"I knew Patton would hire you. He's always been a good boy, and now he's a good man. I'm glad he and Luciano have kept up their friendship all these years." She sighed heavily with nostalgia. "I'm glad my children have a man like him in their lives. I've always adored him."

I had too. "Yes, Mamma, me too." As a teenager, I'd had a pretty major crush on him—not that he or my family ever knew about it. He was ten years older than me, and I'd finally realized that my crush would only ever be just that. He'd never see me as anything but a kid. So, I stopped thinking of him in a romantic way. *But the man has gotten even hotter through the years.*

Growing up, he'd had the thick, dark hair of a teenage heartthrob. As a man, Patton kept it on the neater side even though the unruly waves were impossible to tame completely. The blue of his eyes was enhanced by the thick fringe of his dark eyelashes. He'd always been muscular, and it was nice to see he'd kept up with his exercises. I wondered if all his brothers had also kept in such good shape.

There was no doubt that the Nash boys had been blessed with good genes. But it was Patton's jaw line that really set him apart from his brothers. They all had softer features, whereas Patton's firm, square jaw made him appear tough. It was his eyes that made him approachable. His eyes told of his deep compassion and artistic nature. He was a rare man with many fascinating sides.

"I've just remembered that you're driving through that horrible Austin traffic. You shouldn't be on the phone. Call me once you've settled in. I love you and I'm so proud of you. I know this is the right decision for you. Bye now." And that was that—she ended the call without letting me say a word.

But that was my mother. She wouldn't drive in traffic. Not that she ever had to—we lived on the outskirts of Houston where there was little traffic. She'd drive to the local grocery, the library, and church but that was about it.

My father wasn't much better with traffic. He made it to his job as a supervisor of the cleaning staff at the Conoco Building in downtown Houston. He could drive there each weekday with ease. But if he had my mother in the car with him, he got jumpy. She'd gasp, hold her chest and her breath anytime she saw another car enter the highway—it didn't make her a very good passenger. It was too much for him.

If they wanted to go into the city, Luciano drove them, as he was able to tune out Mother's antics. With the age difference between us, my brother was usually the one to take care of the things our parents needed as they got older.

Mom had been forty when I was born. Being a devout

Catholic, she'd never taken any form of birth control. She'd married our father when she was twenty-one and it had taken eight years before she got pregnant with Luciano. Another nine passed before she got pregnant with me. And I was the last baby she had.

She could have called Luciano a miracle baby too, but for some reason she only called me that. And as a little miracle I had to be protected at all times. Sent to a Catholic school for girls, I was not only kept safe, but chaste as well.

It seemed to be their mission to make sure no male ever touched me—I was their little miracle, and they didn't want anything to tarnish that. It had left me naïve in the ways of love. And as far as sex went, I knew next to nothing. Sex education was not part of the curriculum at the school I'd attended.

"The destination is on your right," the GPS informed me.

Turning into the driveway, I looked up at a nice house that was much larger than I'd anticipated. With only one child, I had expected it to be on the small side. But the deacon's home looked like it could fit a brood of children in it.

There were no cars in the driveway but there was a two-car garage. I tried to avoid blocking it, as I was sure that's where the deacon and his wife would park once they got home.

After I took my luggage out of the trunk, I rolled it up the cement walkway before entering the code into the front door's keypad. I heard it click open and went inside.

The foyer was well-lit by the window at the very top of the—at least—fifteen-foot-high wall. A desk along the far wall had a vase of fresh flowers and a note with my name at the top of it.

Alejandra,

We are pleased that you got the job and happy to have you staying with us. Please make yourself at home, there are drinks in the fridge and feel free to eat anything you want. We're not hard to get along with. Just clean up after yourself and things will be fine.

See you around six,
Deacon and Mrs. Soliz

"So, you got the job then?" a man's voice echoed around me.

Jumping, I gasped, "What?"

Hands shoved into the pockets of his blue jeans, a tall, muscular guy about my age came around the corner. Golden eyes shone brightly as he looked me up and down.

My body went hot as embarrassment filled me. But he seemed to be unaware of my discomfort. "Alejandra, right?" My name rolled off his tongue in a deep, slightly accented purr.

Remembering my manners, I extended my hand. "I am Alejandra De Le Cruz. And, yes, I got the job."

He took my hand but didn't shake it. Instead he turned it over and kissed the top of it as he tugged me closer to him. "I am Alejandro Soliz. It's a pleasure to meet you, Alejandra."

"People call me Alexa." I pulled my hand out of his as I felt my palm begin to sweat.

"May *I* call you Alejandra? It's such a beautiful name, after all." He smiled charmingly as he took a step back. "Allow me to show you around your new home."

I wasn't sure how to take the young man who wasn't supposed to be home. At least, that's what my father had said. "Aren't you going to college at UCLA?"

"I am." He turned, stopping to wait for me to come up next to him. "I've come home for a brief visit. My father's birthday was the day before yesterday, and I came home for the week to be with him."

"How considerate of you." He seemed nice. "You must be very close with your family." Keeping close with family was important to me.

"I am very close to them. I'm their only child, you know." His hand moved to rest on the small of my back and goosebumps pimpled my flesh. "Let me show you to your bedroom so you can put the luggage away."

"Your home is much larger than I thought it would be." I felt lucky he was there to show me around. "I don't think I would've been able to figure out which room is mine if no one was here to tell me."

"Happy to be of service to you, Alejandra." Steering me down a long hallway, he stopped at the last door on the left. "This is my room." He then turned me to the right. "And yours is here, right across the hall."

Something about that made my stomach tighten and I felt as if I were about to break out in a sweat. There were four other doors along the passage, but our rooms were at the very end. It felt a little far away from the main areas of the house to me.

Reaching across my body, he opened the door and moved me inside the large bedroom. Elegantly furnished, the room had two doors, one on the right side and one on the left. "And those doors go where?"

Pointing at the one on the right, he said, "That is your private bathroom and the other one is your walk-in closet." He gestured to the queen-sized bed. "And that is your bed. Would you like to test it out?"

I had no idea what he meant by that, but I wasn't about to go lie down on it in front of him. "That's okay, I trust it's comfortable. This is a lovely home."

He nodded as he took my luggage out of my hand, grazing his fingers along my fingers as he did so. "And large." Rolling my bag toward the closet, he opened the door then put it inside. "Come, I'll show you the rest of the house. My parents' bedroom is all the way across the house." He came back to me as I stood frozen in place.

I had no idea why his words evoked such a reaction in me, but I felt odd. There was a sense of danger mixed with curiosity, and a fair amount of anticipation laced with anxiety swirling inside of me. "So, it's just me and you way down this hallway then?"

"Just the two of us." His hand slid across my side then settled on the small of my back again. "Come."

My feet moved but my mind was telling me to stay put, to lock him out of the bedroom and wait for his parents to come home before daring to come out. But there I went anyway.

I didn't want to come off as some shy virgin. That's exactly what I was, but I didn't want him to know that.

I'd never been completely alone with a man in my life—certainly not one my own age. I didn't know how to act. And for some reason, I had this feeling that this man wanted to have sex with me.

I knew that was preposterous since we were complete strangers, but the feeling just kept building as he continued moving me through the house, talking with his romantic Spanish accent. "The kitchen." He stopped to open the stainless steel refrigerator. "Care for a drink? A glass of wine?"

"I really shouldn't." I'd been allowed a glass of wine only on special occasions. Drinking alcohol with a man present—one who seemed to be highly attracted to me—seemed like a bad idea.

I'd never had anyone be attracted to me. This entire experience was foreign to me. It was a little scary, but also sort of exciting.

3

PATTON

Alexa had been working at the resort for three weeks when her brother could wait no longer and had to come and check on her. We met for drinks later in the evening, as Luciano had gone to the deacon's home for dinner. "Ah, there you are." I stood to greet him.

"It's good to see you, Patton." He gave me a hug before we sat down at a small table.

Waving the waitress over, I ordered him a drink. "Scotch—neat. And I'll take another Guinness." Turning my attention to my oldest and dearest friend, I asked, "So, how'd dinner with the deacon's family go?"

The way his brow furrowed told me that it hadn't gone as well as he would've liked. "Their son is home from college. Did Alexa tell you about that?"

"She did." I didn't think the guy was anything to worry about. "She said they're all very nice."

"I don't like the way he looks at her." Luciano shook his head. "I suppose his parents don't see what I see in their golden boy's eyes. He's lusting after her, Patton. He looks at my little princesa with too much interest in his damn eyes. And she seems as oblivious to it as his parents are."

"Maybe you, being her over-protective big brother, see something that isn't really there, Luci." I thought that was more probable. "She hasn't said anything about him bothering her in any way."

"You don't think she's pretty?" he asked me with wide eyes. "You don't think a young guy his age would be attracted to her?" The waitress brought our drinks and Luci took his, gulping down a large amount of the scotch. He must've felt extremely tense to do such a thing.

"Alexa is gorgeous, you know that." With her shiny, long, dark hair and doe-like eyes, she was a true beauty. "And I can see any man being attracted to her. She's a wonderful person on top of being beautiful. But I just think she would've said something to me if this guy was hitting on her."

"See, I don't think she realizes what he's doing." He took another drink before adding, "He's smooth, Patton. Too damn smooth."

I could see that. Alexa hadn't had much experience with men—she might not be able to pick up on any creepy vibes if the guy was smooth about it. "Perhaps you're right, Luci. She's lived a very sheltered life so far. Why not just have a talk with this guy and let him know that your sister isn't available to be his plaything. It wouldn't be the first time you've done that." I'd witnessed him scaring off a handful of boys who'd had the nerve to come to the door to ask after Alexa.

"If he tells his father that I've threatened him in any way, then I'm afraid they'll no longer want Alexa staying with them. And that would upset my mother, and I don't want that." The mention of his mother reminded me that he'd yet to tell me about her heart condition. "Luci, Alexa told me about your mom's heart problems. Why didn't you tell me about it when it first happened?"

"You were so busy, Patton. I didn't want to bother you with my worries. And she wasn't that bad off. If she'd been worse then I would've told you about it." His smile told me he meant what he'd said. "So, you understand why I don't want to upset her."

"I do." Who wouldn't want to be careful about upsetting their mother if any bad news might kill her?

Huffing, he shook his head. "I don't know what to do. I don't trust that guy. You know he was initially only going to be there for a week? But he changed his plans and is staying for the month now. I think it's only because Alexa is there."

I wasn't so sure of that. "She's working a lot, Luci. She pretty much goes home and goes to bed then gets up in the mornings and comes back to work. I don't think she hangs out with him at all."

"I don't know." He looked away, clearly distracted by his thoughts. "I've just got this bad feeling."

"You're being silly." He and his parents had always been so over-the-top about Alexa. "You have to trust your sister. She's a good person. She wouldn't get involved with a loser."

"I know that, but you said it yourself—she's naïve." He tapped his finger on the tabletop. "That kid is slick. And he's got those pretty-boy good looks, too. I can tell that he's used to having his way with women. And if he has his way with my baby sister, I'll have to kill him."

"So dramatic," I said, trying to remind him that he was prone to being that way over Alexa. "Let the girl live a little. Besides, you can't kill anyone, Luci."

After taking another drink, he put the now empty glass down on the table with a solid thump. "That's not entirely true, Patton. I *can* kill someone. I just can't get caught."

I laughed, having seen this side of him more than once where his sister was concerned. But that was when she was a teenager. "You know that your sister is twenty-two now, right? You know that she's never been out on a date, right? You know that's pretty sad, right?"

Waving at the waitress, he ordered another drink. "I don't see it as being sad at all. I see it as my parents and I have done an excellent job so far of making sure she doesn't get taken advantage of or hurt in some way." He handed his empty glass to the waitress then took the full one. "Thank you, mi amor."

The pretty waitress blushed as she nodded. "You're welcome."

He watched her as she walked away, and the hypocrisy was not lost on me. "So, you can have an active sex life, but your sister can't."

"Don't mention sex and my sister in the same sentence, Patton." He winked at me. "And yes, I can and she can't. She's an innocent baby. You know this."

I didn't know if he'd ever stop seeing her as anything but his little princesa. "She's not a baby. I agree that she is innocent, but not a baby. She's a young woman, Luci. She deserves to get a taste of love—or even just sex—if she wants that."

"Love, I can approve of. Sex with a horny womanizer, I will not." Pointing up toward the ceiling, he went on, "She's a gift from Heaven, might I remind you. One must be careful with such gifts. So, I will continue to be dramatic, as you say, until she's found the right man." He crossed his arms and nodded his head, sure that he was right.

"And that man will love and cherish her the way she deserves," he continued. "He will not even contemplate sex before marriage. He will do everything right with her. We've brought her up to believe in that." Nodding again, he looked like he'd talked himself into something. "Perhaps she *will* thwart this imbecile on her own. She's been taught well and has done as she was told all this time. Maybe I won't have to kill this little pest after all."

"I think you should refrain from saying anything about killing anyone." I looked at a table not too far from ours where a uniformed policeman sat with what looked to be his girlfriend. "We don't want anyone to get the wrong idea."

He followed the direction of my eyes and saw what I did. "Oh, I didn't see him there. Maybe I should calm down a bit."

"I think so. And I think Alexa is a smart young woman. I don't think she'll want to become a notch on any man's bedpost —and I don't think she'd appreciate your attitude about this." I didn't look at his sister the way he and his parents did. I saw her for who she really was. "Since Alexa has come to work for us at the resort, I've watched how she interacts with the staff and with our clients. She's every bit the professional, yet she's personable. Everyone likes her, and they respect her as well. She's really coming into her own."

"That's good to know." A broad smile and a look of pride told me that he meant it. "Everyone has always loved her. She's an angel. But that fool Alejandro Soliz doesn't seem to see her in the right light." The smile faded into a frown as he pulled his glass to his lips. "If his parents hadn't been there, I would've jumped across that dining table and yanked him up by the collar. I wouldn't mind kicking his ass until he promised me he'd never look at my princesa like that ever again for the rest of his life."

There he goes again, going overboard.

"I tell you what—I'll talk to Alexa and ask if she's feeling uncomfortable about staying there if he's going to be home. I can find her somewhere else to stay until he's gone if that's the case. Hell, she can stay with me if she wants to. I'm still in the two-bedroom apartment right now, but the home I'm building is nearly done." I wanted him to know that I was watching her.

Putting his hand on my shoulder, he patted it. "You are an incredibly good friend. I'm glad you're looking out for her. My parents and I thank you very much for all you're doing."

"She's great at her job, Luci. It's a pleasure to have her onboard. You don't have to worry about her." And I didn't think anything was going on between her and the deacon's son either.

"I will never stop worrying about her. I've worried since the day she was born." His eyes clouded over as he sighed. "You know there's a reason we call her a miracle. Mamma only told me some of it, but she had no idea she was pregnant until she gained a lot of weight. She was many months along when she went to the doctor and he confirmed it. But she'd never stopped having her period, so she was confused. When she went into labor, Alexa's heart stopped beating and they had to do an emergency c-section. I know there are far worse stories out there, but that was the worst my mother had ever dealt with."

I had always figured there must be a story there, but that didn't mean they had to safeguard her forever. "Well, she might've had a hard start to life but she's strong now—and smart. She's got her head on straight, too. I do believe it's time to let her do her own thing and stop trying to protect her from the world and every horny guy out there."

"I don't know how to stop," he admitted.

4

ALEXA

I'VE GOT TO BE COMING DOWN WITH SOMETHING.

Stepping out of the ladies' bathroom, I tried to ignore the nausea that had crept up on me that morning. It was nearly noon and I was still having bouts with it.

"Hey, Alexa," Patton called out as he walked toward me.

I'd been looking down and jerked my head up. "Hi, Patton."

Coming up to me, he pointed at my stomach, which I had covered with my hands. "You okay?"

I hadn't even realized I'd been holding myself like that and quickly moved my hand. "Yeah, I'm fine." A burp slipped right out of my mouth, making me turn six shades of red as embarrassment filled me. I threw my hand over my mouth in absolute horror. "Excuse me!"

"Are you sure you're okay?" he asked again as he put his hand on my shoulder. "You can be honest with me, Alexa. This isn't your boss talking, it's your friend."

"I woke up feeling sick to my stomach," I admitted. "But I'm sure it'll go away, and I don't want to leave anyone hanging here at work." After six months of working at the resort, I'd grown very close with my co-workers. I knew they wouldn't be mad if I had to call out sick, but I didn't want to inconvenience any of them.

Slipping his arm around my shoulders, he began moving me toward the exit where employee parking was located. "I'll explain things to your supervisor. I'm going to take you home now. You don't need to be working when you feel sick."

I didn't want to be any more of a bother to him. "You don't have to drive me, Patton. I can drive myself. And thank you for understanding. I think it would be best if I could lie down for a while."

"You go do that. I'll go let Hailey know that you'll be out for the rest of the day. And if you still feel bad tomorrow just call her to let her know that you won't be coming in." He gave me a little squeeze. "If you need anything at all just let me know and I'll be happy to bring it to you."

"I think rest is all I need." It was nice to have someone so helpful around when I had no family nearby. "You're a real sweetheart, Patton."

"So are you. You get better. Call me if you need to." He waved as I walked away from him.

"I will," I called back as I headed out the door and to my car. Now that I was headed home, I wanted to get there as soon as possible. I wanted nothing more than to curl up with a book, a cozy blanket, and a mug of hot tea. That was what my mother had always prescribed whenever I was home sick from school.

Thinking of my mother's home remedies made me realize that it had been a few days since I'd called her. With free time on my hands, I made the call.

"Alejandra?" she answered on the second ring. "How come you're not at work?"

"I'm not feeling well, so Patton told me to go home for the rest of the day."

I couldn't say anything more before she butted in, "Not feeling well? What's wrong? Do you have fever? Sore throat? Is it a problem with your bowels? What is it, my angel?"

"My tummy hurts," I told her. "I keep feeling like I'm going to throw up, but then nothing happens."

"What have you eaten?" she asked, always the problem-solver. I knew she wouldn't rest until she had an answer for my sore stomach. "I hope you didn't eat yogurt. Yogurt has always made you sick. That and watermelon."

I'd gorged myself on watermelon the first and only time I'd ever eaten it. It had been the Fourth of July and we were at a family picnic. I was only ten, and the juicy, tender red meat of the ice-cold watermelon was just about the best thing I'd ever tasted. So, I ate and ate until I couldn't eat anymore. Later that night, I threw up it all up. My mother had dubbed me watermelon-intolerant and that was the end of my journey with the fruit.

Yogurt was a different story. I just hated it, and I'd told her that it made me sick so she wouldn't make me eat it again. "Last night, I had some leftover pizza before I went to bed. I woke up feeling this way."

"That's it then—the pizza. You can't eat leftovers when you don't know if the food was properly cooled before being put in the fridge," she chastised me. "And now you're missing work. That's no good, Alejandra. You must be careful what you eat."

"One day in six months isn't bad, Mamma." I rolled my eyes as I drove out of the parking garage, heading down the street to go to the Soliz's home. "The house will be nice and quiet, so I'll get some rest and hopefully I'll wake up feeling much better."

"Their son isn't home, right?" she asked. "You did say that he went back to college in California, didn't you?"

"He left a month ago." My jaw set tightly as I thought about

Alejandro. "Why are you bringing him up?" I hated thinking about that womanizing pig.

"I just wanted to make sure that he wasn't home and that you two wouldn't be alone in that house together. Your brother doesn't trust him at all."

And Luciano was right not to trust him. Alejandro was a true and complete asshole. I'd found that out the hard way, but at least no one would ever find that out. I had a secret, and I was never going to tell a single soul. "Don't worry, Mamma, I doubt he'll be coming back anytime soon." My plan was to get my parents to agree to let me live on my own so I could be long gone before he ever visited his parents again.

"Good," she said quickly. "Today's the twenty-fifth, so remember to call your Tia Veronica. It's her birthday today."

"Okay, Mamma, I'll call her after I rest, I promise." Turning the corner, I drove down the street as my mother's words registered.

It's the twenty-fifth?

"I'm going over to her house for dinner. We're all getting together to celebrate. I wish you could come, but I know that you can't. We're so proud of you and I'll be sure to tell everyone how well you're doing."

Slowing the car down, I pulled to the side of the road as my head swam. "Yeah, okay, Mamma. You have a nice time and tell her happy birthday for me."

Someone honked as they drove past me. My mother heard the sound. "Alejandra! You're on the phone while you're driving? Chica loca." And then she hung up.

I picked my phone up off the seat to check the date. My brain wouldn't accept that it was the twenty-fifth. But the calendar didn't lie. "Five days late."

How I'd missed the fact that my monthly visitor was late

stupefied me. I was never late—not ever. Banging my head on the steering wheel, I berated myself. "Why? Why? Why did I do it?"

Alejandro had stayed on for the entire first month of my stay at the Soliz's, instead of just the week. He'd hit on me hard and heavy, although never in front of his parents. I wouldn't give into him, as I felt sure that he was only after one thing.

But he didn't leave once the month was up. He told me that he was going to stay to prove to me that he wasn't messing with my head—to prove that he liked me, really liked me.

I still didn't give in—not even a little. He'd tried to kiss me, hold my hand, touch me any way he could, but I never allowed it. He stayed on another month and then another. Five months in all, he'd stayed there, and he'd said he'd done it all for me.

No one had ever wanted me that badly. It was flattering, and he was hot too. I was only human. And so I ended up giving in, and for a week we hit the sheets each night after his parents went to bed.

Losing my virginity wasn't anything like I'd thought it would be. It had been fast, a little painful, and more than a bit disappointing. I wasn't sure how things worked in the sex world, but I did think I was supposed to get some sort of pleasure out of it.

The first time, it took him about two minutes and he was done. I didn't know what had happened until he announced it with a groan, "I came!"

I was left with a mess between my legs and a sense of regret. The next night, when he climbed into my bed, I wasn't into it. He told me this time would be better for me, he'd make sure of it.

I was skeptical but decided to give it another try, only for him to proceed to do things the exact same way as he had the night before. Only this time he shouted out proudly, "I got a nut!"

I had no idea what that even meant, and I wasn't going to ask either. I just rolled out of bed and went to shower. It was becoming clear to me that sex wasn't the be-all and end-all that people made it out to be.

Somehow, I let him talk me into having sex three more nights in a row. Somewhere inside my head, I thought that it had to get better. People wouldn't do it if it was this one-sided. Alejandro just had to put more thought into my pleasure, since I had no idea how to do that for myself. And I told him that.

I went to work shortly after telling him that. And he assured me that night would be all about me. All day long, I thought about what he was going to do to make it better for me. By the time I got home, I was fired up about it.

"Alejandro?" I'd called out as soon as I'd gotten home. I went to his bedroom, excited to find out what he'd come up with. But he wasn't there, and neither were his things.

Later, when the deacon and his wife got home, they told me he'd called them that morning to ask for a ride to the airport. He'd finally gone back to California to get back to his classes.

Stupidly, we'd never exchanged numbers. He'd told me that we had to keep what we'd done a secret from his parents or they'd make me move out. I was fine with that, as I knew I couldn't tell my family either.

"Why didn't I think about birth control?" I kept banging my head on the steering wheel.

Not knowing if being five days late meant that I was pregnant or not, I pulled myself together so I could go to the store to buy a pregnancy test. I had to know. I didn't want to think about what I'd do if it was positive, but if the test showed that I wasn't pregnant I thought that a long prayer to the Virgin Mary would be in order.

As I drove, something told me that I had to prepare myself for a positive test. I had to decide what I would do if I were pregnant. And I knew that I would have to track Alejandro down to tell him we were having a baby.

Feeling everything in my stomach well up at the thought, I pulled over and threw the door open just in time. As I puked my guts up, I tried not to cry and failed miserably.

My parents are going to kill me.

5

PATTON

Hailey came to my office, just as I'd asked her to do if Alexa called in sick again. It would be the third day in a row, and I'd decided I'd make a visit to her if she still wasn't feeling well. "She called?"

Nodding, she leaned against the doorframe, arms crossed. "She said she's still experiencing nausea and won't be coming in today. I told her that you want to speak to her and that you've called her a couple of times. She said to tell you she's been sleeping a lot and that's why she's missed your calls."

Picking up my cell, I called her again. "You just spoke to her, right?"

"I did. I've got a client coming in. If you need anything just shoot me a text." She left as I sat there, waiting to see if Alexa would answer my call this time.

Three rings in, it went to voicemail. I hadn't wanted to bring her brother into things, but she left me no choice. If she was sick this long, she needed to see a doctor. I wouldn't take no for an answer.

So, I made the call I hadn't wanted to make. "Morning, Patton. To what do I owe the pleasure?"

His tone was chipper, and I hated that I was probably about to take all that happiness away. "When's the last time you talked to your sister?"

"I don't like that question at all."

I knew he wouldn't. "I don't like asking it either, if that makes you feel any better. Alexa went home early three days ago with a stomachache and she's called in the last two days, saying she's still not feeling well. I've called and texted her quite a few times in the last two days but she hasn't answered my calls or responded to my texts. So, I'd like to know if she's talked to you or your parents about anything. Is she unhappy with the job? Is that it? Because I won't be angry with her if she doesn't love the job and wants to quit. Or maybe she's really sick and needs to see a doctor, which I'd be more than happy to arrange for her if that's the case."

"Let me call my mother then I'll call you back. I'm not aware of her missing work and I haven't spoken to her. But I will get to the bottom of this, I assure you."

He ended the call before I could even say goodbye. I'd clearly upset him, which was why I'd avoided it. But I couldn't let Alexa sit over there, sick as a dog, and not worry about her.

Or if she wasn't physically sick at all, and just sick of her job, I wanted to talk to her about that too. Maybe she was homesick and hadn't thought about asking for some time off to go to Houston to see her family. Whatever it was, I wanted her to know that I was in her corner.

My cell rang and I saw that it was Luciano. "Well, has she spoken to your mother?"

"Three days ago," he let me know. "She told her that she felt sick to her stomach. Mom said it was from eating leftover pizza. She did say that Alexa has texted her each day, telling her that work is keeping her too busy to call and that she'll catch up with her later in the week and not to worry."

Well, that made me worry even more. "She said she's too busy at work?" I didn't think Alexa was the type to lie—especially not about a thing like that. "Do you suppose she told her that so she wouldn't stress her out?"

"Probably," he agreed. "I was discreet with my mother as well, so she wouldn't suspect anything was off. The last thing we need is for her to get upset. It seems even being too happy can affect her heart. She was at her sister's birthday party the other night and actually passed out when her heart sped up. Dad took her to the hospital, and they said she'll have to go see her cardiologist. She's scheduled to see him sometime next week."

"I'm sorry to hear that, Luci, I really am." I had no idea things were getting that bad with his mother. "Look, I'll go over and see Alexa in person. I don't have the address though."

"I'll text it to you," he said. "I tried calling her but it went to voicemail. Tell her to call me when you see her."

"Will do. Talk to you later." I ended the call then headed to the parking garage. I wasn't going to wait around to see if Alexa would decide to contact me first.

Luciano sent me the address before I even got to my truck, so I put it into the GPS and headed that way. It was only eight in the morning, so I knew I might be waking her up, but I had to see her. I couldn't help but be worried that something just wasn't right with her.

I'd always thought Luci and his parents were over-the-top where Alexa was concerned, but here I was going over-the-top too. Something about her just made me feel as if she needed to be watched over for some reason.

Pulling up to the house, I noticed that her car wasn't there, but two others were parked in the driveway. There was a two-car garage, so her car could've been parked inside of it.

Parking at the curb, I got out and went to the door, ringing the doorbell. A man came to it, opening it as he asked, "How can I help you this morning, sir?"

"You must be Deacon Soliz." I extended my hand and he shook it. "I'm Patton Nash, Alexa's boss and friend."

I didn't like the way he looked at me, with confusion glazing his eyes. "If you're her boss and friend, then you must know that she's not here any longer."

Holy hell!

"I'm sorry—you said she's not here?" I had to have heard him wrong.

"She left three days ago." He turned around and walked to a desk on the far side of the foyer. "Please, come in. I'll show you the note she left for us."

Stepping inside, I felt my heart pounding in my chest. *Something is very wrong here.* "She left three days ago," I muttered to myself. That meant she'd taken off somewhere the day she left work early.

He handed me the note. "See? She said that things weren't working out here and she was going home to her family."

"But she's not with them." I folded the note. "Can I keep this?" I wasn't sure why I wanted the note, but something told me that if we didn't find her, I'd want to have it. Maybe as some sort of evidence. "Thank you for your help, Deacon. If she contacts you, can you please let me know?" I pulled out my business card and gave it to him. "I'm not sure what's going on, but I will find out."

"Check with her friends back home. Maybe she went to one of them, instead of her parents," he offered his advice. "If I hear from her, I will let you know, Mr. Nash."

"Thanks." I left the house I'd been sure I'd find her at, dreading making the next call to her brother..

Getting into my truck, I tried to think hard about any friends that she might've mentioned, either in Austin or in Houston. But

I couldn't recall her ever saying anything about friends in either place.

Alexa was friendly and easy to get along with, but she'd gotten so used to keeping to herself that it had left her from forming any close relationships.

Or has it?

I remembered Luci complaining about the way the deacon's son had looked at his sister. *Could she have been seeing him in secret?*

I knew he'd stayed home much longer than he'd planned to, originally. Five months longer. He'd left to go back to California only a month ago, and I did recall Alexa looking a little upset when she came to work the next day. When I'd asked her if something was wrong, she just said that Alejandro had left without letting her know he was going, and it bothered her that he didn't think to say goodbye.

Could she have followed him?

Getting out of the truck, I walked back up to the door, ringing the bell again. The deacon opened the door. "Yes, Mr. Nash?"

"Your son." I wasn't sure how to put it, but finally came up with something. "Was Alexa seeing your son? As in, romantically?"

Laughing, he shook his head. "No—not at all."

"Were they friends?"

"They got along, but I wouldn't call them friends." He ran his hand over his dark beard as he seemed to be thinking. "Would you like for me to call him to ask if she's there?"

"I would appreciate that very much." Even though her being all the way in California with the guy her brother didn't like would bother Luci in many ways, at least we'd know where she was.

Taking out his cell, he made the call. "Good morning,

Alejandro. I know it's very early, but I have a gentleman here who is looking for Alexa. He wanted to know if she's with you or if you've heard from her. We think she may have left here to go be with a friend somewhere." He went quiet as his son gave him the answers I hoped would help me. Then he just shook his head. "I see. Thank you, son. Go back to sleep."

"He hasn't heard from her?"

"Not at all. He said she doesn't have his number or his address, so she couldn't be with him. And he said they weren't close enough for him to even consider them friends."

"Thank you, sir. I'll get going now." I turned to go back to my truck, not knowing how Luciano would take the news that I hadn't found out anything except that she'd left the Soliz's.

Driving away, I made the call, gritting my teeth. I knew his reaction would be bad. "What did she say?" he answered my call.

"Nothing." It wasn't a lie.

"What do you mean nothing?"

"She wasn't there, Luci. The deacon gave me a note she left for them three days ago. It said that things weren't working out here and that she was going back home."

"Son-of-a-bitch!"

"Yep." I thought the same thing. "I had him call his son, too. He's back in California. I thought maybe she and he had had a little romance going on in secret and maybe she went to him, but she isn't with him."

"Thank God," he said with relief.

"He said they weren't close enough to be considered friends. So, I guess that means she never let her guard down with the Lothario. I told you that you could trust her to use her own judgment."

"Patton, her judgment where that rat is concerned may have

been good, but what about what she's doing now?" He had a point.

"Yeah, this isn't like her." I didn't like it at all. I didn't want to bring up foul play, but something wasn't right.

"I'm going to text her to let her know that I'm now aware that she's left the deacon's home and that I know about the note she left too. I'll give her a few hours to contact me or I'll be forced to go to the police. That should smoke her out of hiding."

"Toss in the thing about your mom passing out and having to go to the hospital. Twist that guilt card." It wasn't like me to think that way, but I was worried about the girl.

"Whatever it takes to make her tell me where she is, I will do it. You did say that she's been calling into work, right?" he asked.

"She has been doing that, yes." At least that meant she was alive. "I just don't know where she would have gone. And I don't know why all the lies either."

"Me neither. But I will find out. There's gotta be something wrong, Patton. My princesa doesn't do things like this."

I had to agree with Luci there. It only made me more curious about why she was doing so now.

6

ALEXA

Driving to Los Angeles, California, my only passenger was the little stick in a clear baggie sitting in the seat beside me. It was there to remind me of the importance of getting to Alejandro.

After purchasing a pregnancy test, I'd gone home and taken it. Finding out that I was pregnant nearly killed me, so I knew it would do the same to my mother. If I could tell them that I was getting married to Alejandro and then a month later tell them that we were pregnant, it might lessen the blow. But I had to find out if the father of my baby would do the right thing.

I'd found his phone number and address in the desk in the foyer at the Soliz's. I didn't call him to give him the heads up about my coming. I wasn't sure how he would react at all. But I prayed that he would accept the fact that we'd gotten pregnant together and that he'd take his share of the responsibility.

It had taken me three days to get to L.A. I'd stopped and spent the nights in motels, instead of trying to drive straight through. I didn't want to be tired and endanger the little baby growing inside of me. Already, I felt love for it. I hoped Alejandro would learn to feel it too.

"Turn left here," the GPS told me. "The destination is on your left."

Apartment 115. I took a deep breath, grabbed the little baggie with the positive pregnancy test in it, and got out of the car. The early morning hour might've seemed a bit too early to deliver such news to a man, but it also meant he'd almost certainly be at home. At six-thirty in the morning, I rang the doorbell to his apartment.

My heart raced, my stomach did flips, and my head went fuzzy as I waited for him to open the door. The sound of the chain sliding filled me with relief. *He's opening the door—so far so good.*

The open door came to a stop and a woman stood in front of me, wearing nothing more than a t-shirt that hit her at the waist and a tiny pair of black panties. Her blonde hair was a mess, and she rubbed her eyes. "And just what the hell do you want this early in the fucking morning?"

"Is Alejandro here?" I hoped I had the wrong apartment.

"Geez, this motherfucker is getting all types of woken up this morning." She stepped back then walked away, leaving me at the door. "Alex, get the fuck up. Some chick's here for you."

He'd told me once that he never went by anything but Alejandro. Seemed he'd lied to me. And it seemed that he lived with the foul-mouthed woman who'd answered the door as he shouted back at her, "Baby, I don't want to see no other woman but you. Get your fine ass back in this bed and tell the slut to hit the bricks," his thick Spanish accent was gone.

He faked that too?

"She's holding a bag with a pink pregnancy test in it, Romeo. Get up and deal with that," she yelled as she went into the hallway, disappearing into the darkness.

"She's holding a what?" I heard him say.

"Alejandro," I shouted from the doorway. "It's Alejandra. Please come talk to me."

"Alejandra?" he asked, sounding confused. "From Austin?"

"Yes. Please come talk to me." I found everything about him unsettling at that moment. He'd have to change drastically to become a good father. I'd had no idea he was this sort of man.

Pulling a shirt on as he came out into the living room, he'd managed to put on a pair of blue jeans but had yet to zip them up. "What the hell are you doing here? How'd you get my address?" He pulled up the zipper of his jeans then buttoned them. "My father called a little while ago, asking me if you were here. So, what are you doing?"

"Your father called?" I'd left the Soliz family a note that said I was going to Houston to my family. "Why'd he ask if I was here?"

"Apparently, someone went to his home looking for you." He came outside, closing the door behind him instead of inviting me to come inside. His eyes went to the bag I held, and he just shook his head. "I don't know what made you think to come here. I'm not going to do a thing about that, except tell you to get rid of it."

My heart stopped and I clutched my stomach. "What?"

"Get. Rid. Of. It," he reiterated. "I don't know why you think I even want to know about this problem. I left without telling you for a reason. I lost interest. So, what makes you think that coming to me with news of a baby is going to make me feel any differently?"

"*You* made this baby." I wasn't even sure I wanted him in the child's life now. "I can't believe the son of a deacon would even entertain the thought of getting rid of an unborn child."

"I assumed you were on birth control," he said with a sneer. "It's the girl's job to take care of that so she doesn't have to take care of a baby on her own, you know."

"You lied to me. You told me you cared about me. You just said whatever you had to say to get me into bed. You stole my virginity. Do you even care?" I couldn't even look at him. The sight of him made me sick inside.

"Guys do that kind of thing all the time, honey." He shoved his hands in his pockets, shivering in his bare feet in the cool morning air.

"For five months?" I didn't think all guys waited around for that long just to get into a girl's pants.

Smirking, he chuckled. "I'd never had a virgin before. I thought it would be worth the wait. You were tight and all, but you were also frigid as fuck."

"You didn't even try to turn me on. You just went for it. And you want to blame me?" I held up the baggie, shaking it in his face. "I didn't enjoy the sex either, if you must know. But that doesn't matter at all right now. All that matters is that sex gave us a baby. I will never get rid of this baby—even if it has a donkey's butt for a father. It's not this poor child's fault that I believed in you, Alejandro."

"No, that's all *your* fault." He looked up at the sky as color began to show out of the darkness as the sun started to rise. "Get back in your car and go back to your family. I'm not about to claim that thing. For all I know, you've been screwing other guys since I left."

"I have not!" I couldn't believe him. "I'm not that kind of girl."

"You might be telling the truth. You certainly aren't good at sex. But that changes nothing." He pointed at my car. "Go home, Alexa. I don't want you anymore and I will *never* want that thing inside of you."

"Alexa?" He'd never called me that. "Does calling me that help you disassociate me from the woman you chased after for nearly half a year?"

"Goodbye. Don't come back here and don't go to my parents either. I'll just tell them that you're lying, and they will believe me." His lips slowly curved into a sinister smile. "Better yet, if you tell my parents about this, then I'll tell yours. My father has your father's phone number. It won't be hard for me to fuck up your life."

I'd never wanted to punch someone in my life, but my hands fisted of their own will. I wanted to wail on him. "You're a horrible person, Alejandro Soliz!" It became clear to me how stupid I'd been to drive all this way. He would be a terrible father. "I won't tell them because I've changed my mind about you. I don't want you in this baby's life. This child is mine and mine alone. Forget I ever came here. Forget my name and forget that you have a child."

"I already have." He turned and walked inside; I heard the chain sliding into place as he locked me out.

Tears stung the backs of my eyes as I ran back to my car. I had no idea what I was going to do, but Alejandro would not be a part of it. "How am I going to tell my mother this news without it killing her?"

I got into the car, tossing the baggie onto the passenger seat again. I'd left my cell phone on the seat and it lit up when the bag hit it. I saw there was a missed call from my brother, and a text too.

Wiping the tears from my eyes, I read the text:

"I don't know what you're doing but if you don't call me by noon today, I'm going to tell the police that you're missing. Mom doesn't need that, and you know it, so you'd better call me ASAP!!!"

My hands shook as I swiped the screen to call him before he involved the police.

"Finally!" he answered the call. "Do you have any idea how worried I've been? Patton is sick with worry too. I've yet to inform our parents about what you're doing." He paused before asking, "What *are* you doing, Alexa? And where the hell are you?"

"I'm in California." I gulped back a sob.

"California?" he sounded confused. "Patton had the deacon call his son there only about a half hour ago. He said you weren't there. Who else do you know in California?"

"Only him. Only Alejandro."

"And why would you go all that way to see him? Why would you lie to the deacon and tell him you went home to our parents? I don't understand what's going on, Alexa. This isn't like you."

I opened my mouth to tell him why I was acting so crazy, but only sobs came out. I couldn't stop crying. I didn't know what I was going to do. I couldn't upset my mother. I couldn't bear to think of the way my father would look at me if I had to tell him that I'd made a horrible mistake and allowed someone I didn't even love to take my virginity.

I could barely hear Luciano telling me to calm down as I cried loudly. I needed help. I had no idea what I would do on my own. So finally, I managed to get out the words. "I'm pregnant, Luciano."

The line went silent. I knew he was disappointed in me. I knew he was angry with me. He must've been as lost as to what to do as I was.

"Come home, Alejandra. Not to Houston. Go to Patton's. We can't upset Mom right now. She has an appointment with her cardiologist next week. She passed out at Tia Veronica's birthday party the other night and had to be taken to the hospital."

"Oh, no!" I straightened up, wiped my eyes, and then started the car. "I'm coming back now. It'll probably take me another three days to get back, Luciano."

"Share your location with me, Alexa. And answer my texts and calls. I'll let Patton know you're coming home."

I didn't want him to tell Patton about my pregnancy. I was deeply ashamed. But before I could tell him to keep my secret, he ended the call.

Pulling onto the street, I felt odd. I'd never done anything I was ashamed of before. It felt horrible. And soon everyone would know what I'd done. Looking back over my shoulder at the apartment where Alejandro was, I knew then that no matter how hard you pray, God can't change the heart of a snake.

7
PATTON

My sweating palms had my hands slipping on the steering wheel. I'd never been so worried about anyone in my life. If Alexa weren't so innocent and naïve, I wouldn't have been this anxious. But my mind kept running away from me.

What if someone has abducted her? What if she's fallen for some shady man who's talked her into running away with him? What if I never see her again?

My cell phone dinged, and I looked at the screen to find that Luci had sent me a text message. Grabbing the phone, I read it quickly as I sat at a red light:

"I found her in California. She's coming home. She said she'll be back in Austin in three days. I told her to go to your place. Can you send me the address of your new house? I'll come tomorrow to tell you more."

"California?" I began driving again, breathing a lot better now that I knew she was okay and coming home. "To my home?"

I'd moved into my new house a couple of weeks ago. There was ample room for Alexa to stay with me but I had to wonder why Luci would want her to. Something had to have gone on at the Soliz residence.

I'd seen the deacon call his son that very morning, and he'd said that he hadn't seen Alexa. I had no idea who else she knew in California. If not Alejandro, then who? And why run off without telling a soul what she was doing?

My guess was that Alejandro had lied to his father. Thank God Luci had scared Alexa into telling him where she was. She had to have run away to be with Alejandro.

But if that was the case, then why had she agreed to come back? And why wasn't she going to be staying with Alejandro's family if they were a couple? And why was I so wrapped up in what she was doing?

Nosing around in someone else's business wasn't like me. I didn't give unsolicited advice. I didn't stick my nose in where it wasn't wanted. And I knew for a fact that Alexa didn't want my nose in her business, or she would've told me where she was going.

Pulling into the parking garage at work, I thought about how she'd had a stomachache the day she left. *Was that just a lie to be able to leave work early to head out to California?*

She could've told me what she was going to do. It wasn't like I would try to stop her or anything. It must've been because she hadn't wanted her brother to know her plans.

I would have to have a serious talk with my friend about how his over-protective ways only made Alexa feel like she had to lie to so many people just to be able to have a boyfriend. She and Alejandro had obviously lied to the deacon and his wife as well. I didn't know if that was because Alexa wanted it that way or if it was Alejandro's doing, but they'd hid their relationship well from his parents.

As I got out of the truck, I shook my head, trying to rid it of my thoughts. I had no evidence at all to support my speculation about Alexa and Alejandro's relationship. I was jumping to conclusions—another thing that was nothing like me.

As I walked into the building, I saw Hailey and waved at her. "I've got news on Alexa."

She came toward me. "Oh, yeah?"

"Yeah. She's not at home. She's not sick." Luci hadn't told me that part, so I corrected myself. "Well, I don't know if she's sick or not. But I highly doubt it since her brother found out she's in California."

"What's she doing there?" she asked with a frown. "And why did she think she had to lie to me? If she wanted to take a vacation all she had to do was ask for one. Do you think she wasn't aware of that, Patton?"

"I really don't know. But I do know that she's due back in Austin in three days, and I *will* find out. Are you cool with me letting her come back to work if that's something she wants to do? As her supervisor, it's your call to make.

"She's been great up until now. I'd hate to fire her." Her furrowed brow told me she had to give it some thought.

"Well, you think about it and let me know. You've got three days to make a decision." I didn't want to play favorites with Alexa, especially if she was going to be lying and disappearing again. "I've got work to get to."

"Me too." She turned to leave. "I'll let you know what I decide before she gets back. I don't think firing her is the right thing to do, I can tell you that right now. But this shouldn't go without some type of reprimand."

"I agree." I wasn't going to let Alexa get away with being so deceitful. Mostly because there just wasn't any reason for her to deceive me or her supervisor. But she'd never had a job before, so I didn't know what she thought she had to do in order to get some time off.

The next evening, I sat at home watching football on television when my doorbell rang. I'd been expecting Luci to show up at any time, so I jogged to the door to answer it. "Hey, old friend."

"Hey, Patton." He came in, shoulders sagging, and I'd never seen such a haggard expression on his face. "Please tell me that you've got some scotch here. I need a drink like I've never needed one in my life."

"I happen to have a bottle." I went to the bar off the living room and made him a drink as he sank into a chair. "You look awful." I handed him the glass then went to take a seat on the couch. "Is your mother doing okay?" His hang-dog expression couldn't possibly be over his sister. She was coming back, after all.

He took a long drink before answering me. "Mother is doing okay at the moment. She had the appointment with the cardiologist yesterday. There are still some tests that have to come in, but the general diagnosis is heart failure."

"That sounds bad, Luciano." I wasn't sure what exactly that diagnosis entailed, but the idea of one's heart failing sounded just about as unhealthy as it could get.

"It's not good, my friend. The doctor says she's got class three congestive heart failure. No one wants her to get to class four, as that would mean she'd have trouble breathing even when sitting or lying down. For now, she only has issues when she's up doing things for too long of a time."

"What are they doing for her?"

"Giving her medications to see which ones will work best for her. The main thing is eliminating stress. And let me tell you, that is the hardest thing to do. Life has a way of making stressful situations that cannot be avoided." He took another drink, his hand shaking as he pulled the glass to his mouth.

"Well, at least Alexa won't be giving your mother any stress since she's on her way back here. So, I'm dying to know why the hell she went all the way to California and why she thought she had to lie to me about it." I leaned over, picking up my beer off the coffee table as I waited for him to fill me in on.

His chest rose and fell as the lines in his forehead deepened. "Well, it seems that she and that little prick did have a relationship."

"I knew it." My first instincts were spot on. "So, she went to see him. But why didn't she think she could tell me about that? I would've given her the time off to do that. She does have vacation time. Do you think she just didn't understand that?"

Shaking his head slowly, he went on, "I think her head was a mess when she left."

"Why?" I asked, perplexed. "Was he breaking up with her or something?"

"No." He took another drink then said, "She told me that they hadn't communicated at all since he left. See, he left without telling her goodbye or giving her his number."

"So, she snooped around the deacon's house and found his address?" I didn't think that sounded like her at all.

"She told me she found his address and phone number in the desk in the foyer." He took another drink, his lips forming a thin line as anger filled his eyes. "You see, she had to find him. She felt she had to give him the opportunity to do what's right."

"What's right?" I knew of only one thing that went along with a term like that. "Did she and he? Did they? Oh, shit!"

Nodding, he agreed, "Oh shit, indeed. Alexa told me that Alejandro hit on her hard and heavy for five months. He kept telling her he wouldn't go back to California because he cared for her and wanted her. Finally, she gave into the constant pressure. They hooked up for about a week, then one morning she went to work and when she came back, he was gone. His parents told her that he'd called them at work and asked if they could give him a ride to the airport; he was ready to return to school."

With her sheltered upbringing, it wasn't hard to guess that she hadn't used protection. "She's pregnant."

"That, she is. She took a pregnancy test right after leaving work sick that day. Once she had the positive test, she became desperate to get to the father to seek his help." Gulping down more of the amber liquor, he sucked in his breath then said, "That bastard doesn't want anything to do with her or the baby. And she said he's not who she thought he was anyway. He's living with some girl in Los Angeles. She wouldn't want him to be in the child's life anyway. He's a horrible person."

I was glad to hear that she wasn't going to try to hang onto the guy just because of the pregnancy. "I don't want you to worry, Luci. She's got a great job and she can stay here while I find her a place of her own. I'll make sure she can afford the rent on her salary. And she's got medical insurance too. Plus, we've got a small daycare center at the resort that's free for both guests and the staff. Alexa will be fine."

His dark eyes slowly rose to meet mine. "Yes, I know she will be fine, my friend. It's my mother who I'm worried about. If she finds out that her little angel—her miracle—has not only had sex out of wedlock, but is also about to become an unwed mother, it will kill her. She won't live to see the face of her grandchild."

I hadn't thought of that. "Damn, Luci. That's a terrifying thought."

"Extremely. And that is why I am going to ask you to do something that I never thought I would have to. Not in a million years did I see this coming."

I had no idea what more I could do for him or Alexa. But he was one of my oldest and best friends. "Just ask, Luciano."

"Will you marry my sister, Patton?"

8
ALEXA

I'd been gone a total of six days by the time I pulled back into Austin. Luciano had assured me that everything was going to be okay. I was to go to Patton's new home on the outskirts of town, and he'd fill me in on everything.

I hadn't lost my job, so that was a plus. I would most definitely need it to cover my expenses with the pregnancy and the baby.

I'm going to be a mother!

Rubbing my belly, I couldn't help the joy I felt that there was a little one growing inside of me. I didn't care that its father was the worst man on Earth. I loved the little baby unconditionally. And I hoped my mother would somehow find it in her to love her unexpected grandchild too.

Luciano had told me that he'd come up with what he thought would be a foolproof plan about telling our parents about my condition. He said they would even be happy about it. For now, though, I wasn't to even hint at my news when speaking to Mom. And that proved hard to do, as we'd had some long phone calls as I drove back.

I had to hide the fact that I was driving so much from her.

She couldn't know that I'd taken off to go to California, or else she'd be upset. My brother told me that her condition had gotten worse, so I knew I had to watch what I said to her.

Being alone for the last six days hadn't been easy, with so much weighing on my mind. I was looking forward to the day when I could be honest about my baby with others. It was a very strange time in my life. I was ecstatic about the baby, yet sad about the baby's father being such a jerk. And I was sad about how my mother might be affected by the news. I wanted her to be as happy as I was about it. But I knew that wasn't going to happen. At least, not at first.

I had prayed that the idea of me being a single mom would grow on her. I had a great job that would allow me to keep the baby at work. There was a daycare at the resort, so I wouldn't ever be too far away from my little bundle of joy. I was going to be okay.

Things could've been much worse, and I hoped my mother would see that. I wasn't some helpless teenager. I was twenty-two; I'd be twenty-three by the time the baby came. The only thing I had to do between now and then was to get myself a nice home. My baby deserved a nice place to live. I would make sure my child never wanted for a thing.

As I crossed the border into Austin, I put Patton's address into the GPS. He'd moved into his new house a few weeks back and I'd never been there. Being able to stay with him while I looked for my own place meant a lot to me. He was a great friend to my brother, but also to me.

He'd given me a dream job, and now he was going to help me out while I got my life together. Patton Nash was a godsend. I wasn't sure how I would repay him for all he'd done for me, but I would find a way to show him how grateful I truly was for all of his help.

Luciano hadn't told me what he'd told Patton about why I'd

left or my situation. I supposed my brother wanted me to explain my actions to Patton on my own. Which was okay. It would be a difficult conversation for me, as I'd never dreamed that I would have to tell him such intimate details about myself, but there were worse things in life, so I couldn't complain.

The GPS took me to the entrance of a suburban community that led me around through a maze of gorgeous homes. Finally, it told me to stop in front of a set of iron gates with a huge letter N in the middle of them. "Wow." The home behind the gates was amazing—the star of the entire neighborhood.

I hadn't realized how wealthy Patton had become since opening the resort with his brothers. He'd never acted like he had tons of money. He was still the same old guy he'd always been—a real sweetie with a heart of gold.

Looking at the texts my brother had sent me, I found the one with the gate code and punched it in. The driveway was smooth as glass as I drove up it. The lawn was lush, green, and manicured to perfection. Tall oaks that had to have been hundreds of years old flanked each side of the driveway.

The two-story home with off-white natural stone siding looked welcoming. Parking near the front door, I got out. My legs felt like jelly, as I knew the time had come to open up to Patton about things that I never thought I'd be saying to him.

Before I could ring the doorbell, the door opened and there he stood with a welcoming smile on his face. "You're home."

"My home for now, thank you very much." I wasn't sure why he had a huge smile on his face. But then it occurred to me that my brother must've told him everything. Blushing with embarrassment, I ducked my head, staring at the ground and not knowing what to say.

His fingers caught my chin, pulling my face up to look at him. "You're not the first or the last young woman to be duped by a charismatic jerk. There's no reason to be embarrassed about what happened."

Staring into his blue eyes, I liked how soft and non-judgmental they were. "I feel like an idiot."

Reaching out to me, he pulled me into his arms, hugging me while rocking me back and forth. "Don't feel like that, Alexa. You're not an idiot. I can't imagine being able to hold someone off for five months—especially since you lived with the guy."

"It wasn't easy." Patton's words—and his hug—gave me comfort and a sense of being cared for. I needed a little of that after the mean things Alejandro had said to me. "What hurts the most is that he lied about everything he ever said to me. Seeing him in California... it was like he was a completely different person. He'd been completely fake with me. And he's got the wool pulled over his parents' eyes too."

Releasing me from his embrace, he took me by the hand and pulled me along with him into the living room. "Some people are masters at being fake. Much like a chameleon that changes its colors to blend into their surroundings, some people have that same ability to hide from their prey. It doesn't make you an idiot to fall victim to someone like him."

He sat me in a comfy chair then walked away, giving me a chance to look around at my stunning surroundings. "This is a gorgeous home, Patton. You've done an amazing job."

"Thank you." He went behind a bar made from a dark red wood. "I wanted everything in the house to come from somewhere close by. This bar was hand-carved out of a solid piece of mahogany wood by a craftsman right here in Central Texas. The rocks that make up the exterior siding come from a dry riverbed about ten miles from here."

I had to get up to take a closer look at the piece. Running my hand over the shiny surface, I thought that I'd never seen anything like it. "It's a work of art, Patton. Not just a bar at all."

There must've been a mini fridge built into the back of the bar, as he leaned over then came back up with a frosty mug of milk and a muffin. "Here, you need a little snack after your long ride home. I've got a rack of lamb in the oven for dinner, but that won't be ready for another hour or so."

I was hungry, and very grateful for his forethought. "Thank you, Patton. That sounds yummy. I've never had lamb before, but I think I'll love it." I took a bite of the bran muffin then a drink of milk as he came around the bar, taking a seat on one of the overstuffed barstools. I climbed up on the one next to him, continuing to eat the muffin.

"Luci and I have talked extensively about how it would be best to deliver your news to your mother in a way that won't stress her out. We don't want to give her any more heart problems than she already has." He drummed his fingers on top of the bar.

"Have you come up with anything yet?" I finished off the muffin before draining the remnants of milk from the glass. "Man, I scarfed that down, didn't I? I guess I was a lot hungrier than I realized."

"You should get used to that idea—you'll really have to up your caloric intake. I've been doing some reading on it. We want you to have a healthy pregnancy—for you and the baby." He stopped drumming his fingers then took my hands in his, pulling me around to face him. "Alexa, your brother and I have come up with an idea that we think is best for everyone."

I was eager to hear what it was. "So, tell me already. I'm dying to know what the plan is. It's killing me not to tell Mom. Though it didn't happen in the best of circumstances, I do consider this great news. I know this baby won't have a father, but it will be loved."

"It *will* be loved." He licked his lips. "And it will have a father, Alexa."

I wanted nothing to do with Alejandro. "Look, I don't want my brother or you making Alejandro marry me, or forcing him to be a father to this baby. He's not a good person, Patton, and I don't want to share this baby with him. Biological father or not, he's not someone I want in my child's life."

"I agree," he said, confusing me. "He won't be the one who will be this baby's father. It will be *me*, Alexa."

I wasn't following at all. "I don't understand. Are you saying that you and my brother think my mother won't be stressed out by this, so long as she thinks you're the one who got me pregnant? I can assure you that she will be just as upset about me having sex out of wedlock with you as with anyone else. So, that's not a good plan." I'd been so hopeful, too.

"That's not the entire plan." He gave my hands a gentle squeeze. "You and I are going to get married right away."

"No!" To say I was stunned was an understatement. All I knew in that moment was that I couldn't let him do that much for me. "Patton, no!"

"Listen to me, Alexa." He seemed to have prepared himself for my reaction. "It will be a legal marriage, but it won't be a real one. It's going to be a marriage of convenience, like people used to have all the time. After the baby is born and things have settled down, we'll get a divorce. But I will always take care of you and the baby, at least financially. And I'll always be this baby's father. This way, you won't upset your mother, and you also won't be trapped in a marriage with a man you don't love. One day, you will get to marry a man you fall in love with."

"I'm already about a month along. She'll know we lied when the baby comes in eight months, instead of nine." I wasn't sure about this plan at all. It seemed too crazy. "And what about you, Patton? This fake marriage might stop you from finding a woman you love. What if you miss out on Mrs. Right because you've tied yourself down to me—even if it's not for that long?"

"I'm not worried about that. I am worried about your mother though. We'll only have to stay married for about a year. That's not too much time out of my life—or my love-life—to sacrifice for a woman like your mother, Alexa. Your family was always there for me after my parents died. I can spare a year for your mother."

Though I was overwhelmed by Patton and Luci's plan and had a lot of questions, there was one thought that stuck in my head: *I would be a fool not to marry this man.*

9

PATTON

"Okay, Alexa," I coached her as we took an Uber from the small airport nearest her parent's home in the Houston area, "we're in love. We've been dating seriously for the last three months, but we've been seeing each other since shortly after you came to Austin. It's important that we both stick to that timeframe or your parents will know something's not right."

"I know." She wrung her hands in her lap, clearly nervous. "This is just going to be so awkward, Patton."

That was the one thing it definitely could not be. "You have to pretend that it's all true or your mother will see through us, and we can't have that." Luciano would be at his parents' home as well, to make sure they knew that he was in favor of our marriage. "You know, your brother is having to lie too. We all are. But you have to remember why we're all being deceptive."

"Mom," she whispered as her eyes clouded over. "I can't let this kill her." Wiping away the unshed tears, she nodded and gulped. "I can do this for her." Smiling, she looked at me with something akin to adoration in her dark eyes. "Patton, I don't know how to thank you enough for the sacrifice you're making for me—for my family, and this baby." She ran her hand over her stomach. "I'll never be done repaying you."

I didn't want her to think she was indebted to me. "Alexa, I'm doing this because my heart told me to. Because helping you is the right thing to do. I don't expect a thing in return." Shrugging, I thought she should know how I really felt. "I'm thirty-two. Not ancient by any means, but I'm not some young, dumb kid either. I know I can be a good father to your child. And I'm ready to be that."

"Do you honestly feel that way?" she asked with a furrowed brow full of worry. "Because I don't think you've had enough time to fully digest this whole thing. How can you be sure that you're ready to become a father?"

"I'm not into running around anymore. I love my work and my life. And I do believe that having a child in my life will be an amazing experience." I thought about how that sort of left her out of things. Reaching over, I took her hand, giving it a gentle squeeze. "Plus, I think sharing a child with you will be an amazing experience."

Her wide eyes told me she was much less certain of this plan than I was. "How can you be sure of that?"

"I've known you since you were born. We've spent more time together than I've spent with any other woman on this planet. If things had been different, I probably would've been like an uncle to this kid anyways," I smiled at her, trying to lighten the mood before becoming serious again. "We've always gotten along well, and we know one another on a deep and personal level." I had to let her know how I felt about her, so she'd be able to trust that we'd be able to raise a child together. "I respect you, Alexa."

"And I respect you, Patton." Her smile made my heart skip a beat. "You and I will make awesome parents."

"I know we will." Pulling into her parent's driveway, the time had come to put on a great show for them. "Are you ready for this Alexa? I'll be holding your hand a lot, hugging and even kissing you. Not on the mouth, as I'd never do that in front of your family, but on the cheek. And you can kiss me on the cheek too. We have to make this look real."

The Uber driver parked the car then looked at us as we sat in the backseat. "Wow. This is by far the weirdest conversation I've ever overheard on the job. Good luck with everything—you're going to need it."

Getting out of the car, I felt a little embarrassed that someone else had heard everything we'd said. "Thanks for your discretion."

"Sure thing."

Helping Alexa out of the car, I heard her mother opening the front door. "They're here!"

Alexa had called her the night before to let them know we'd be coming for a visit. Her parents hadn't even asked why I was coming along. I'd been like a part of their family for so long, they must have thought it was normal that I'd join Alexa on her trip home.

Running to her mother, Alexa wrapped her arms around her. "I've waited too long to come see you, Mamma."

"You have, my errant daughter." Her mother hugged her back. "But we are so proud of you for working so hard, so your father and I aren't upset with you for not coming to see us sooner." She let her daughter go then held her arms open for me. "And Patton, so nice of you to come."

Hugging her, I felt a twinge of guilt, as I knew the lies were about to begin. "It's so nice of you to have me."

We all headed into the house, where we found Luciano and Mr. De La Cruz standing to greet us. Luci wore a broad smile as he hugged his sister, pretending they hadn't just seen each other the day before. "My, my, you're growing up, Alexa."

I was sure he'd thrown that in there to remind his parents that Alexa was no longer a child. "She has become quite the young woman," I added. Shaking her father's hand, I went on, "Your daughter has made a name for herself at the resort already. Many of our repeat clients ask for her directly."

"That's wonderful news," her father said as he glowed with pride. "Whatever one does, they must do it well or it's not worth a dime."

"I agree." Looking at Alexa, I took a deep breath, preparing myself for what was to come. "Are you ready?"

Nodding, she came up beside me, looping her arm through mine. "Mom, Dad, we have something we'd like you to know."

I was afraid she was about to jump the gun, so I cut in, "You see, when Alexa came to Austin and we began working together each day, we began seeing each other in a different light than we had before. As you can see, your daughter has grown into a true beauty—both inside and out. She's a remarkable woman, with high moral values."

Alexa broke in, "And Patton is a wonderful man, who I respect immensely. And we've spent a lot of time together."

I watched her mother's eyes dart back and forth between us. "Are you two dating?" she asked in a near-whisper.

Luci came up beside his mother. "Just so you know, Patton talked to me about dating Alexa before he ever asked her out. They've had my approval for months."

"I see," Mrs. De La Cruz nodded as a smile began to curve her lips. "What do you think, Papi?" she asked her husband, who stood on the other side of her.

Mr. De La Cruz eyed me then laughed and clapped his hands. "I think this is great news. There is no better man for our daughter than this one right here!"

Joy spread through me that things had gone even better than I'd thought they would. Hugging Alexa, I whispered in her ear,

"At least they're happy about us. Only one more hurdle to make."

She kissed my cheek and it surprised me, as it made a small jolt of electricity zap through me. "Finally, the secret is out, mi amor." She hugged her mother and father. "I'm so glad you approve."

"How could we not approve of our darling Patton?" her mother asked. "He's such a wonderful man."

Another shot of guilt burst through me as her mother sang my praises and grinned at me. I tried to ignore the feeling—I was only doing it for the sake of her health. "And your daughter is a wonderful woman."

Throwing her arms around me again, Mrs. De La Cruz hugged me tightly. "You have made me so happy, Patton."

After a wonderful dinner, Luci, his father, and I retired to the den for a drink. Luci nudged me as we followed behind his father. "I think this will be the perfect time to ask him."

"You don't think this will seem too fast to him?" I was worried that we were rushing things.

Luci cocked one brow at me as he gave me a funny look. "Time is of the essence here."

He was right about that. Every day we waited to get married would make it more obvious that Alexa had been pregnant before we wed. "Good point."

His father poured us all a glass of Scotch, and when they sat down, I stayed standing. His father eyed me. "You seem to have something on your mind, Patton."

"I do, sir." Putting the glass down on the side table, I tried to get ready to ask a question I had never seen myself asking before. "Mr. De La Cruz, you know that I have the utmost respect for you."

"I do." He took a drink, watching me over the rim.

"Since your daughter and I have been dating, I have treated

her with the respect that I know you demand. I've never stepped over the line with her, sir." I'd rehearsed the speech in the shower that very morning, but the words were lodging in my throat, as it felt as if it were closing up on me.

Is this the right thing to do?

Lying to Alexa's father felt wrong. So wrong that my body seemed to be trying desperately to stop me from doing it. But I looked at my best friend and found his eyes begging me to continue.

Mr. De La Cruz put his glass down. "That is welcome news, Patton. I thank you for letting me know that."

Gulping, I had to go on. "I've fallen in love with your daughter, sir."

"I can see that." He smiled. "The way you act with her told me as much. You're very delicate with her."

I had tried to be, and apparently the limited amount of touching we'd done throughout the visit had worked to make her parents believe that we were in love. "I adore Alexa. And I know that there is no other woman for me, sir."

Nodding, he smiled. "She is a rare gem, isn't she?"

"The rarest, sir." I pulled the small box out of my pocket and opened it to show him what was inside. "I bought this for her recently. Before I give it to her, before I ask her the question, I want to ask you if you approve of me marrying your daughter?"

For a long moment, he sat there, staring up at the ceiling, then he looked at me with shining eyes. "I wholeheartedly approve of a union between you and my daughter, Patton Nash. Nothing would make me happier." He held up one finger. "That's not entirely true. One thing might. I would like to witness this proposal so I can see my daughter's eyes when you ask her this important question."

I hadn't seen that coming, but seeing Luci nodding out of the corner of my eye told me I should go with it. "How about I ask her right now?"

Standing up, Mr. De La Cruz was all for it. "Then let's go see what the women are doing in the living room."

When all three of us walked into the living room, both Alexa and her mother stopped talking. Her eyes were on me. "Are you gentlemen through with your drinks already?"

"We are," her father said as he took his usual seat in his recliner.

Luciano took a seat on the sofa as I walked to where Alexa sat in a chair. "Honey, I've got something important to ask you." I got down on one knee, clutching the box in my hand as guilt flowed through me like a river gone wild.

I wasn't an actor, so none of this came natural to me. But one look at Mrs. De La Cruz, holding her hands over her mouth as tears ran down her cheeks, turned me into an Academy Award-caliber leading man. "Alejandra Consuela Christina De La Cruz, will you do me the great honor of becoming my wife?" I popped the lid open on the box, showing her the ring she'd already seen and had even tried on when we bought it before setting off to see her family.

Holding out her shaking hand, she whispered with a quiver in her voice, "I would love to marry you, Patton James Nash."

As I slid the ring onto her finger, something flashed inside of me, causing my body to become white-hot. I wasn't sure what it was, but figured it must be guilt mixed with excitement.

I stood, pulling her up with me to hug. I looked down at her as tears rolled down her cheeks. "I love you, Alexa. You've made me an incredibly happy man."

Sobbing, she buried her face in my chest as she clung to me for dear life. "I love you too, Patton."

Luciano came to us, wrapping his arms around us. "I'm so

happy for you both. You have no idea how happy you've made this family."

More arms wrapped around us as their parents came to join the group hug. I felt welcomed into their family in a way I'd never been before. And it was all because of a lie.

I had to get over this, so I shook my head to clear it. "Now, for my next surprise. Alexa and I will be taking off within the hour to go to Las Vegas to get married as soon as possible."

"Are you serious?" Alexa asked with surprise—even though this was no surprise at all to her. We'd discussed the trip along with all of the other lies we had to tell.

"I am completely serious. I want to make you my wife before the sun leaves the sky tomorrow evening."

The sooner this wedding is behind us, the better.

10

ALEXA

SITTING DOWN ON THE SOFA IN OUR HONEYMOON SUITE AT A RITZY Vegas hotel, I didn't know how to feel. I didn't know what I was supposed to do. I didn't know how I should act.

Looking at the wedding ring on my finger—the one that matched Patton's—I began to feel suffocated. The marriage was real now, legal, legitimate in every way. The love wasn't there though, the passion wasn't there, and the knowledge that he and I had only gotten married to spare my mother any stress overwhelmed me.

The wedding ceremony had happened less than an hour ago, yet it was a blur to me already. The Elvis impersonator who had officiated our wedding must've gotten the right answers out of me, as the one thing I could recall was hearing him say, "You can now kiss the bride, you hunka hunka burnin' love."

That's when Patton took both of my hands, pulled me to him, and then pressed his lips onto mine. The numbness I'd felt all day had ended in an instant as fireworks went off inside my head and my heart nearly beat out of my chest. I'd never experienced anything like it. The kiss left me floating as he swept me off my feet, carrying me out of the little white chapel then up to our suite.

Patton wanted to give me everything I'd have from a real wedding. He'd bought me a gorgeous and expensive wedding dress made by *the* Vera Wang. Vegas had it all, and anyone with tons of money could get the most fabulous clothes on the planet within hours.

Patton had purchased an entire ensemble of clothing for me for our honeymoon. He said we had to have lots of pictures to make things look real to my parents.

"You look amazing." He snapped a picture of me sitting on the sofa then began putting the camera on a tripod. "I've told you that, right? You really do look the most beautiful I've ever seen you." He chuckled playfully. "Marriage suits you, Mrs. Nash."

Cocking my head to one side, I had a hard time understanding how he was so cool and confident. "Patton, you know what we just did, right? We just got married—for real. You're no longer a single man, and I'm no longer a single woman. For now, we're bound to one another in a way neither of us ever saw coming. It's a little mind-boggling, right?"

"You can't think like that. We've done what needed to be done." He straightened his tie then ran his hands over his black suit. He'd gone with a black suit made by Tom Ford and looked like a model wearing it, too. "Time for some pictures."

He came to me, holding out his hands. "I'll put you on my lap. It'll look playful."

Sitting on his lap was new for me. I couldn't recall ever doing it—not even when I was a kid. But there were photos to take, so I got up and let him move me the way he wanted to. "Should I maybe put my hands on your cheeks, and we can look into each other's eyes—or something like that?"

"Sounds nice to me." He waited for me to get into place. Our eyes met and he clicked the clicker in his hand. "That's going to be a good one. And now, how about one with us kissing?"

My stomach got tight and my lips tingled. My body remembered how it felt to kiss the man who was now my husband. "K."

"I'll let you make the move, Alexa. Move in when you're ready to." His blue eyes searched mine. "Are you okay with doing this?"

My heart melted with how sweet he was. "I can honestly say that kissing you has been far more enjoyable than any of the kisses I shared with that jerk."

His laugh sounded good to me. "That's good to know."

Moving in, I closed my eyes because looking into those azure pools of his made it hard to concentrate. Slowly, I came to him until our lips touched. I heard the sound of him taking the picture and then I heard nothing except the popping of fireworks that once again went off inside my head.

I'd thought the crush I'd had on him long ago was over. But the way it felt when we kissed had me rethinking that. It was even a bit overwhelming. When our mouths parted, my breathing was on the ragged side.

I'd wrapped my arms around his neck while we kissed without realizing what I was doing. His hands ran up to take mine then he pulled my arms off him. "I think those pictures will look real."

Probably because that felt real.

It started to crop up in my head why they called them crushes. Because you end up feeling crushed when you realize it's one-sided. So, I pulled back a whole lot. "I'm hungry, are you?" I climbed off his lap, needing to put space between us.

"I've made reservations for us at Picasso." He got up and went to the bar, filling a glass with white wine for himself and then pouring me a sparkling water. "You should go change into the pale blue Elie Saab and the Jimmy Choo Viola sandals. The ones with the crystal embellishments." A sudden grin came over his lips as he added, "I've stashed a gift for you in the bag with the shoes. Wear them too."

"Patton, you've bought me too much already. You don't need to be giving me gifts as well." It felt wrong for him to keep gifting me with things. The whole thing was fake, after all.

"We have to make it look good, my dear wife." He sipped his wine before going on, "A man who loves his wife wants to give her things. Now go change so we can get to the restaurant."

I found the dress in the closet and then the bag with the shoes in the bottom of it. When I pulled out the shoebox, I saw another box had been slipped into the bag.

The large, square shape let me know there was some kind of jewelry inside. Nothing could've prepared me for what I found when I took the top off, though. Sparkling diamonds dripped off of a silver chain. Matching earrings were inside with the necklace. I couldn't breathe, as I knew I held something in my hands that was worth more than my car.

After changing clothes, I put the jewelry on then looked at myself in the full-length mirror. "Who am I?" I ran my hands down the floor-length dress. Moving one foot, I let the sparkling sandal show. "I am Mrs. Patton Nash, that's who I am." Giggling, I thought about all the times I'd pretended I was married to Patton when I was in my early teens. Looking into my eyes, I couldn't believe how things had come about. "This isn't real, Alexa. You must remember that above everything else. This is *not* real."

A knock came at the bedroom door. "Are you ready? We don't want to be late."

"Coming." I made my way to the door then opened it.

His eyes went wide and his jaw dropped. "You—um, damn, girl—you look—well, uh," he stammered. "Okay, I'll just say it. Alexa, you look sexy as hell."

Blushing, my entire body heated. "You picked all this stuff out. I just put it on." Looking into his eyes, I had to let him know one thing, "You've got great taste, by the way." I fingered my necklace. "Thank you for the jewelry, it's the most beautiful and expensive thing anyone has ever given to me."

He ran his hand over my shoulder, whispering huskily, "It all pales in comparison to your beauty, Mrs. Nash. I mean that, too. I don't want you to think that I'm saying these things for any other reason than that I mean them. After all, there's no one around that we're trying to fool right now."

Patton had never looked at me the way he did just then. I wasn't sure what that meant. He'd said before that the marriage wouldn't be real. But what did that really mean?

I had the idea that he did expect some things to be the same as they were in a legitimate marriage—and in that moment, I was perfectly fine with that. "Patton, I will be a good wife to you, I promise you. I will be all a wife is supposed to be."

Blinking, he seemed stunned for a moment. "We're not going to have sex. I would never expect that of you—would never do that to you, Alexa."

Not even if I ask nicely?

11

PATTON

We spent the night having dinner, dancing, and snapping photo after photo to post to our social media accounts. We tagged her parents in all of them. All in all, we'd truly outdone ourselves. But all our kissing, hugging, and touching had done a number on me. "I'll sleep on the sofa." I jerked my head toward the door to the bedroom. "You take the bed."

"I feel bad," she said with her pretty red lips downturned. "I'm smaller than you. I'll fit on the sofa just fine."

Grabbing the handle underneath the sofa, I pulled it out to show her that it turned into a bed. "I'll fit just fine."

Shaking her head, it seemed she wasn't about to give in. "I can still take this bed. You're the one paying for this expensive room. You're the one who's doing so much for me and this baby."

I thought I'd stop her right there. Walking over to her, I took her hands in mine. "Alexa, we should probably start saying that this is *our* baby, not just yours. Not only for your parents' sake, but for this child's sake as well."

Her eyes glistened as she smiled a little. "Ours? Are you sure you want me saying such a thing?"

I found it funny that she wasn't getting the gist of things yet.

"Won't it be mine? I mean, I will sign the birth certificate as the father, and the child will carry my last name. It's no different than if I were to adopt a child—it'll be mine in every way that matters."

Pulling one hand out of mine, she ran it across my cheek, gazing at me with wonder. "You're something else, Patton Nash. Mamma calls me her angel—I'm beginning to wonder if you're not mine."

I didn't want her to think of me that way. Taking her hand off my face, I held it once again. "I'm no angel, Alexa. I'm just a man who has a deep respect and love for your family. I don't want to see anything happen to your mother, either."

Nodding, she pulled away from me then turned around. She went to the closet and pulled some pillows and a blanket off the top shelf. "You are an angel, Patton." She came back, tossing the pillows on the sofa bed. "And a hero."

I took the blanket from her, spreading it out on my bed for the night. "I am not. And *I* am going to sleep on this bed. It's nowhere near as comfortable as the one in the bedroom. I want you to sleep on that one and I won't take no for an answer."

Shrugging, she knew she'd been beat. "I had a wonderful time tonight. Even if it was all fake. Thank you." She kissed the palm of her hand then blew it at me. "Have sweet dreams, mi amor. I know I will. See you in the morning."

"I guess that's going to be the term of endearment you'll use with me?" I liked it. "I'll stick with the old go-to, you'll be babe." Watching her nod as she left the living area, my heart, head, and cock all shouted at me to go to her, pick her up, and take her into that bedroom and make her my wife for real. But then her brother's face filled my mind. *I will not betray my best friend.*

Going to the bathroom, I took off my suit then started the shower. The night had been wonderful, and it hadn't felt fake to me at all. I found Alexa beautiful, charming, and fun. I didn't want to be attracted to her, but it seemed impossible not to be.

All night, her silky dark hair had hung in loose waves around her gorgeous face. Her doe-like eyes had sparkled the whole time we were out. And her body felt good in my arms when we danced. I kept finding one reason or another to dance with her, and we found ourselves on the dance floor again and again.

The hot water felt good as it ran over my skin. Closing my eyes, I imagined that the tiny trails of water that ran down my body were her fingertips. *What would she do if I went to her, naked, wanting—needing her?*

I had to wonder if she was as attracted to me as I was to her. But the one thing I knew for sure was that she and I were not in love. Luciano would never forgive me for taking his sister to bed unless we were in love—and maybe not even then.

He'd come to me because he knew he could trust me not to hurt his sister. He trusted me not to do anything unacceptable with or to her. And I knew exactly what he considered to be unacceptable.

Sex was top of his list, of course. She was also not to be talked down to. I knew. He would never tolerate anyone laying a hand on Alexa in anger. And she had to be respected as a person at all times. To him and his family, she was a gift from above, and everyone was to treat her that way.

I didn't see her quite the same way they did. I didn't see her as some porcelain doll that had to be handled as if she might break at any moment. I did see her as a respectable woman—her own woman. I did see her as a beautiful woman. And now I'd begun to see her as a desirable woman.

But that's the one thing I can't see her as.

As much as I kept telling myself that Alexa was off-limits, the combination of my drifting thoughts and the water on my skin made me feel amazing in a way they never had before. The heat heightened my senses and my skin tingled as the water pelted my back.

Soaping up my hands, the plan was to get washed and get the hell out of the shower that was making me think about Alexa in ways I shouldn't. But, as with anyone cleaning their naked body, my hands moved down to where my hard-on just wouldn't give up and go away.

I needed to get rid of it. But not while thinking about Alexa. Trying to picture the last woman I'd had sex with a few months back, I got her face in my mind then went for it.

She'd been okay. We didn't have enough of a spark to keep seeing each other though. And soon her face faded away and was replaced with Alexa's.

My dream Alexa willingly moved into my arms, straddling me as I picked her up effortlessly. Her legs wrapped around me and she let her head fall back as she moaned with pleasure. "Yes, mi amor. Show me what it means to be your wife."

Kissing a line along her neck, I pressed her back against the wall, ramming my hard cock into her soft, warm, wet pussy. "Being my wife means you'll get this hard cock every single night. Being my wife means I will treat you like the queen you are. Being my wife means you will never be alone in anything."

Her nails dug into my back as I moved with force. I had one mission—to please her. And please her I did. "You're the most amazing man," she moaned with passion and desire. "You're powerful, handsome, and the best lover I've ever had."

"You're the best too." I took her mouth, forcing my tongue through her slightly parted lips. Tasting each other, our tongues ran around together playfully. I took her ass in my hands, lifting her to fit me better. Soft, tender, and ripe—she was ready for what I had to give her. "I'm about to fill you up with my seed, wife."

"Do it, mi amor. Fill me all the way up with your hot seed. Give it all to me. I want all of you." She wiggled, making me go in even deeper.

Nipping her ear, I whispered, "I want you to have my baby." Cum shot out of me as my eyes flew open, bringing me back to reality. There I was in the shower, alone. But the words had actually come out of my mouth.

I'd never had an orgasm that left me feeling guilty. At least not while I was jerking off. I'd come too fast in my younger days, and those times had left me feeling bad for the girl I was with. But alone? Never.

Shutting off the shower, I didn't know why my fantasy had taken that direction. First of all, Alexa was already pregnant with another man's baby, and nothing would change that. Second, I wasn't ever going to be intimate with her—not ever. Third, the honeymoon needed to end—and quickly.

I couldn't keep doing things together like we had that day, or I would eventually end up doing something I would deeply regret. Something that could cost me one of the longest relationships I'd ever had.

I can't let this affect my friendship with Luciano.

He'd asked me to marry his pregnant sister because he trusted me with one of the most important people to him. And I would have to find a way to tamp down the growing attraction. I had to nip it in the bud.

There was no way I could ever say those things to Alexa. She would think I was a fool, for one. Plus, it would make her feel bad about herself. Giving herself to that idiot had been the stupidest thing she'd ever done. Probably the *only* stupid thing she'd ever done. Reminding her of that in any way would just be mean.

Wrapping the towel around myself, I wiped the steam off the mirror to look at my reflection, and then I looked at the wedding ring on my left hand. I'd bought matching wedding bands, which went with the engagement ring I'd given her.

We looked like the real deal. We looked like newlyweds. But we were a lie, a farce. We were nothing more than two people who'd known each other forever, trying to pretend that we'd gotten married out of love for one another. And we were expecting a baby.

Smiling, I thought about how happy her mother would be when Alexa told her about the baby. My heart swelled with joy at the knowledge that I'd played a key role in why her mother would be happy when she told her about the baby, instead of heartbroken and sick.

It would all be worth it to see that. Worth the lies. Worth the nights of having to hold myself back from the growing feelings I had for Alexa. It would all be worth it in the near future.

But then there would be a divorce to go through, and that would be hard on Mrs. De La Cruz. Being devout Catholics, the De La Cruzes didn't believe in divorce. But they knew that I wasn't nearly as devout as they were. *Don't they?*

Going out to the living room, I took off the towel then climbed into bed, naked. Thinking about religion, I wondered how Alexa viewed divorce. *Will she balk when it comes time to end this marriage? Will she use her religious beliefs to try to keep this marriage going? And what will I do if she does that?*

12

ALEXA

Not long after arriving back home in Austin, I'd just finished putting away the clothes Patton had bought me in Las Vegas when I heard the doorbell ring. I made my way across the large bedroom to see who was at the door.

I stopped in my tracks as I heard the voice of Patton's oldest brother, Baldwyn. "What have you done?"

"How'd you hear?" Patton asked him.

I opened the door just a crack so I could hear them better. Baldwyn sounded upset for some reason, and I wasn't about to bust in on them. But I did want to know what had upset him.

"I called Mrs. De La Cruz to ask her how she's been doing. I guess you didn't know that I check up on her sometimes, because she told me something that I couldn't believe. I thought she had to be talking about a different man named Patton. But nope—she was talking about you."

"You didn't say anything, did you?" Patton sounded worried.

"About what?" Baldwyn snapped. "About you and Alexa *not* dating? About you and Alexa *not* being in love? About you and Alexa *not* getting married?"

"We got married," Patton told him. "Yesterday."

"What the actual fuck, bro?" A puffing noise told me Baldwyn had sat down heavily on the sofa.

Patton hasn't told his brothers about our fake marriage?

I don't know why this surprised me, but it did. Knowing that Patton had done all this behind his brothers' backs had me thinking that he'd made the decision to marry me too quickly. He hadn't asked a word of advice from even his oldest brother.

"Look, keep your voice down—I don't want Alexa to hear you."

"She's here?" Baldwyn asked. "In your home?"

"She *is* my wife," Patton said with a chuckle. "So, yeah, she does live here now."

"I am so lost right now that I can't even begin to tell you. Just please tell me that you had the forethought to get her to sign a prenup."

"No, I didn't ask her to do that. I'm always going to take care of her, Baldwyn."

"Why is that?" Baldwyn sounded perplexed. "She's your best friend's little sister! I'm sure Luciano doesn't like this at all."

"He's the one who asked me to marry her," Patton dropped the bombshell.

"Are you fucking with me, Patton? Because if you are, it's not funny at all. You have no idea how confused I am. I mean—hell, I feel like I don't even know who the fuck you are right now. Getting married is a big deal. And you just up and ran off to Las Vegas and got hitched, *for real*, without telling anyone but *her* family about it? Why? I've got to know why you would do something so completely stupid."

Leaning against the wall, I felt sick to my stomach. I had never realized that Patton's family would have an issue with our marriage. Guilt built up inside of me. To be honest, I hadn't thought about his family at all.

I'd done this to myself and now Patton was paying the price for it.

"There is an incredibly good reason that I have married Alexa, Baldwyn. I'm not a stupid man. I have great respect for her family. You know that."

Baldwyn huffed. "What does that even mean, Patton? If you respect them so damn much, then why did you marry their daughter—a woman you have *not* been dating? A woman you do *not* love?"

"She's pregnant, Baldwyn," he finally came clean.

There was a long moment of silence before Baldwyn asked, "With *your* baby?"

"No." I heard the sound of Patton pacing across the living room, his heels clicking against the tiled floor. "The guy who did the deed has fled to California and wants nothing to do with her or the baby."

"So, what does that have to do with you? Tons of women have babies without the fathers in the picture, Patton. You didn't *need* to marry her. This isn't the old days where a woman's scorned for having a baby out of wedlock," Baldwyn argued.

"Her mother has a pretty bad heart condition. But you are aware of that, aren't you? I mean—you have talked to Mrs. De La Cruz, right? So you would have to know about her health issues."

"I do know about it," Baldwyn said. "She didn't mention a pregnancy though."

"She doesn't know about it yet," Patton told him. "We hurried to get married because Alexa is only one month along. This way, we can tell her parents about the pregnancy in about month, and they'll be happy about it instead of upset."

"And when this baby shows up a month early, then what?" Baldwyn asked.

"Babies do that sort of thing all the time. It won't be a big deal. You'll see," Patton sounded confident, and I hoped it would make his brother feel better about everything.

"You do realize that she's got you on a string now, right?" Baldwyn asked him. "I mean, she's got you on the hook for at least the next eighteen years and probably longer. And then you'll also be expected to pay for this kid's college, I would guess."

"Look, I want to do this," Patton said, sounding angry. "And I'm not about to argue with each one of my brothers over this. That baby will be mine in every way but one. Not that our child will ever be made aware of that."

"So, the marriage is real, and it'll last?" Baldwyn asked. "I mean—you've gotta know that the De La Cruz family won't be keen on you two divorcing. You get that, right? You're married to someone you don't love. And you're sort of stuck in this now."

"I'm not stuck in anything," Patton shouted. "I know what I'm doing."

"Hey, you told me to keep it down and look who's yelling," Baldwyn cautioned him. "And what about how Alexa feels about having to live with you and be married to you? This has to be freaking her out. She's like a little sister to you. This isn't right, Patton, and you know it."

"So, one minute she's got me by a string and the next I'm molesting her?" Patton sounded exasperated. "For your information, I haven't touched her. And I won't."

A sense of disappointment rumbled inside of me with his words. I'd had many dreams about him as I slept in our honeymoon bed— alone and untouched. The attraction I felt toward Patton was only getting stronger. But it sounded like it was still one-sided.

"Do you think I don't have you on social media, bro?"

"The pictures were meant to make her parents believe in our

marriage and our love. So, yes, we did some kissing, hugging, and touching for the camera. It wasn't real."

Sagging against the wall, I felt weak in the knees. It had felt so real to me—so real and so right. But not to Patton.

Is this marriage a huge mistake?

"It looked real, Patton," Baldwyn informed him. "The stars in your eyes don't lie."

"It was the lights. And we had to make it look good."

"And what about the glow that surrounded Alexa in those pics?" he asked. "How'd you fake that?"

"She's pregnant," Patton replied. "Pregnant women glow all the time."

"If she falls in love with you, then what will you do?" his brother asked.

"Baldwyn, we have no idea what the future will hold. I know that my friendship with her brother is what matters to me over everything else. He and I have been friends since we were little kids. I will not betray the trust he's put in me."

Another wave of disappointment hit me to join what was already there. Patton was a respectable man, and his friendship with my brother would stop him from ever being able to see me in a romantic light. I had to stop dreaming about the man in that way. I had to stop thinking stupid thoughts, like that one day we'd have a real marriage and become a real family.

"You and Luciano should've come to me with this. You shouldn't have made this decision alone. Now you've got this poor girl married to you. How do you think she really feels about that?" Baldwyn asked.

"I think she's happy that her mother will be happy about his baby, instead of the news possibly killing her," Patton snapped. "This isn't about me. It's not about Alexa, either. It's not even about the baby. This is about the life of a woman who has done a lot for me. You know how much Mrs. De La Cruz did for me after Mom and Dad died. She was the one who held me close and made me feel like I had a mother in her. I didn't feel so alone anymore. I didn't feel like a goddamned orphan, thanks to that woman and her husband."

Tears filled my eyes. I'd never known that about him. I knew he felt comfortable with my family, but I didn't know that he saw my parents in that light. And that made me feel even worse about the dilemma I'd created.

I'd made a huge mistake, and Patton's devotion to my mother had him making one too. He didn't love me and never would. He wouldn't allow himself to fall in love with me—for my brother's sake.

But I couldn't change a damn thing. I couldn't tell him to annul the marriage or it would kill my mother. I had no control over this anymore.

"Patton, I'm sorry for coming down so hard on you about this. I know you love that family. But I am seriously concerned about Alexa. Don't you think she deserves to find a man whom she loves and loves her back?"

"Of course she deserves that. And when the time is right, we'll end this marriage so she can be free of me and free to find real love. Until then, we will continue to make this marriage look real to everyone. We will share this child, Baldwyn. It will be a Nash. And that won't ever change."

"You don't feel as if you'll be doing an injustice to your eventual bloodline by doing that?" Baldwyn asked. "You will eventually have kids of your own and a wife you really love. How do you think this little fiasco will make them feel?"

"Who knows what the future holds?" Patton asked. "All I know for now is that there is a woman who needs me to be a father to her baby. There is a baby who is going to need a father, and I intend to be that father in every way. This will be my firstborn child, Baldwyn. Get used to it."

His words made my heart soar. Running my hand over my flat belly, I whispered, "He will be a great father. You have nothing to fear, little one."

"And what about being a husband to its mother, Patton? How will you be that for her when you won't do the things a woman needs from her husband? I know your heart's in the right place, but this will end badly. One of you will eventually end up having sex with someone else or something like that, and that's when things will crash down on you both."

"Sex isn't everything, Baldwyn. I can do without it." Patton got quiet before adding, "For a year, I can do without it. We'll see what happens when the urge hits me. But you don't have to worry. I'll always be honest with Alexa."

"So, you think that telling her that you'll be screwing some other woman won't bother her?" Baldwyn laughed. "You're living in a false reality, bro."

"Do you think I'm not aware of that?" Patton asked. "This isn't normal, and it feels that way. But I've committed myself to Alexa and our baby."

"*Her* baby," Baldwyn corrected him.

"*Our* baby," Patton said with force. "This is *our* baby. Not just hers. And I don't want anything ever said to this child about it being otherwise. If you can't accept that, then you and I will be having some issues."

With a heavy sigh, Baldwyn got up, his footsteps going toward the front door. "I can see that I'm not going to get anywhere with you, Patton. This will never play out the way you think it will."

"Oh, yeah?" Patton asked. "And how's that? Because I haven't thought about how it will play out at all. The only thing I have thought about is that *I* will be this child's father, legally. And I won't ever turn my back on Alexa or our child."

The sound of the door closing told me his brother had left,

and I couldn't stop myself from running out to Patton. I threw my arms around him, tears pouring from my eyes. "Thank you! Thank you so much!"

"I'm sorry you heard that." Hugging me tightly, he kissed the top of my head. "We will get through this, you know. People will get used to it. They always do." He let me go then turned away, his shoulders slumping a bit.

It only made me care for him more. I could already see the weight he carried on his impeccably broad shoulders—all because of me and my decision to trust an untrustworthy man.

13

PATTON

"I know you're nervous, Alexa." I reached over to take the hand she'd been twisting in her lap as we sat in the examination room, waiting for the obstetrician to come in. "It's to be expected. This is your first real exam."

"Are you sure you want to be here for this?" She gulped as she looked at me with wide eyes.

"I'll stay right here by your side. Don't worry, the doctor will drape you before checking your..." I struggled to find a word—other than vagina.

"Yeah, I know." Her cheeks flooded with color. "I just mean that you don't have to do anything you don't want to do, Patton. I'm already asking for too much from you as it is. Going to all the boring doctor's appointments is going above and beyond even that."

"I want to be here with you." I meant every word of that.

Having a fake marriage was turning out to be harder than I'd expected. It was extremely difficult for me to convey my feelings to her. I'd been able to hide my attraction to her during the day because work separated us most of the time. When we were home, there was dinner to cook and clean up and then we'd go our separate ways to our own bedrooms. But the attraction was still there, nonetheless.

"You're a good man." Her breasts rose and fell with a sigh.

"And you are a good woman."

"Not really." Her head dropped. "What I did was irresponsible."

"The one irresponsible thing you've ever done," I reminded her.

She chuckled, but it wasn't a happy sound. "And I had to go and make it one of the worst things a person can be irresponsible about!" It was clear to see that she'd been beating herself up over getting pregnant.

So, I thought I would try to lighten her up a bit. "Well, I'm excited about becoming a father. Once we have the news from the doctor, we can tell your parents, and then we can start working on the nursery. I've got tons of ideas that I want to work with you on."

Her eyes lit up. "You mean, you and I will work together on the nursery?"

How can she think that I'd leave her out of that? "Of course. We'll work together on everything that has to do with our child."

Nodding, she looked back down as her feet dangled above the step she'd used to get up onto the examination table. "Are you thinking about using animals in the theme or shapes? Or what about trees and flowers?"

"Actually, none of those things." But I was glad she was bringing up some ideas. "You know me and my flair for interior design—classic, bold, with a splash of Texas in everything."

"I like teddy bears." She smiled. "Do you like them?"

I smiled. "We can incorporate them into the design." It occurred to me that we hadn't done much talking since we'd gotten back from Vegas. We'd been married a month already, and the time had gone by with us not communicating much at all.

I knew I needed to change that. "You know, you and I need to start acting like a family if we want our kid to have a good home life. I think we need to do more than eat dinner together at night then go our separate ways."

A smile curved her full lips as she looked at me. "That would be nice, Patton. I enjoy spending time with you, I truly do."

And I enjoyed spending time with her too. It was the physical attraction that worried me. "I like spending time with you too, Alexa."

A quick knock came on the door then the doctor opened it and walked in, a small laptop computer open in her hand. "Just got the results of the pregnancy test back and looks like you two *are* going to be parents." She placed the computer on the counter then looked at us, obviously gauging our reactions to the news.

"That's awesome news," I said as I pulled Alexa's hand up, kissing it. "Hear that, babe? We're going to be parents."

Tears slipped down her cheeks. "I heard that." I let her hand go so she could wipe away the tears.

"Well, congratulations, you two." The doctor approached her to start the exam then, listening to her heart, checking inside her ears and mouth. Then she turned away and went to get something out of one of the drawers. "Go ahead and lay back, Mrs. Nash. It's time to do the pelvic exam."

Alexa's eyes closed as she lay back. I ran my hand over her head, knowing she was nervous about this part of the visit. "It's going to be okay. I'm right here for you, babe. Do you want to hold my hand?"

She held up her hand and I took it. "Thank you, mi amor."

The doctor looked at me as she turned back around with a big silver thing in her hand that looked like it could cause some pain. "Aww, that's so sweet. I like that." She moved Alexa's feet into the stirrups on either side of the table then tossed a blue sheet over her bent knees to cover her from view.

I'd been researching a lot about pregnancy and parenthood, but I hadn't read much on what happened during a woman's pelvic exam, so I had no idea what the doctor was going to do with that thing in her hand. I watched as she pulled out some sort of lubricant and slathered it onto the silver thing.

I couldn't take my eyes off it. My stomach got tight and my head got light. "What's that?"

The doctor held it up. "This is a speculum. We insert it into the vagina so we can take a look around."

Alexa's eyes flew open, landing on the contraption that was about to be inserted into her. "What do you need to see in there?"

I thought I'd been alarmed by the device, but Alexa looked damn near frantic. "It's okay, babe. I'm sure the doc here knows how to be gentle with that thing."

A smirk came across the woman's lips as she muttered. "I'm a hell of a lot gentler than most men who go poking around in there."

Alexa looked at me with red-stained cheeks and wide eyes. I ran my hand over her head as I held her shaking hand in the other. "Just close your eyes and this will soon be over."

Sitting on a little rolling stool, the doctor grabbed a huge light then pulled it around to shine it on Alexa's privates. When she turned the light on, I went blind for a moment. "Let's see what we have here." I couldn't see exactly what she was doing, but by the way Alexa's hand tightened around mine, I got the idea that the silver thing was being inserted.

I heard a weird cranking noise and had to ask, "What's that sound?"

"Me, opening up the speculum," she said as if it were nothing at all. But then she looked up at me, directly at my dick. Shrugging, she went back to work.

As I stood there, feeling a little like a piece of meat, I thought about what she must be looking at. A tight, inexperienced vagina—one that hadn't been touched in two months now.

Alexa's voice shook as she asked, "Is everything looking okay?"

"Yes." The doctor's head popped up over the sheet as she looked at Alexa. "How long have you two been together, may I ask?"

Now I was *sure* she was wondering how in the hell this young woman had such a tight little vagina when she'd been having sex with a man like me. So, I answered that question, "We've been dating for six months but we've only been having sex in the last couple of months."

She smiled at me politely but looked a bit confused by my answer. "Oh, well, it's good to know you're not having any problems in that department." I could feel my cheeks getting red, realizing I had let my imagination get the better of me.

"So you've only been together six months?" She looked at Alexa and then at me. "I'm not one to pry, but this baby is going to make your marriage harder than it is right now. Many new parents find that couple's therapy can really strengthen their relationship and help with the transition to parenthood."

After imparting that advice, the doctor reached over to grab an exceptionally long cotton swab out of a jar full of them. Waving it around, she said, "Get that therapy and get into the fun of having a new marriage, you guys. It'll help your connection grow." She moved her hand in a way that told me she was now inserting the cotton swab.

Alexa growled, "Ow!"

"Sorry, this part is a little uncomfortable sometimes," the doctor agreed. "But I've got to get a sample to send to the lab for testing. We want to make sure you don't have anything wrong going on with your reproductive cells." She put the cotton swab into a vial then sealed it. "And that's a wrap, folks." She cranked the silver thingy then pulled it out and slung it into the sink. "You can get dressed now and my office will give you a call when the results from the pap smear are in."

Alexa leaned up on her elbows. "I thought we might get to hear the baby's heartbeat today."

"At two months?" She shook her head. "It's a bit early for that." She looked back and forth at us. "But you know what, let's give it try."

My pulse quickened at the thought that we'd get to hear the baby's heartbeat for the first time. "Thanks, doc."

"Not a problem." She pulled up Alexa's shirt before smearing some more of the lube onto a flat thing that hung around her neck. Placing it on Alexa's tummy, she noticed the goosepimples that rose on Alexa's arms. "This is cold." She put the end pieces of the device into her ears and listened.

"It sure is." Alexa shuddered as she looked at me with a perplexed expression.

"Oh, yeah, I got something here." She turned on a machine beside the table and then grabbed something else that she coated with the lube before placing it on Alexa's stomach. "Listen up."

Soft whooshing filled the small room, and I knew what I was listening to immediately. "That's it."

Tears ran down Alexa's face. "The heartbeat. It's so fast."

"It's so strong." I leaned over and kissed her on the forehead. "Just like you."

Alexa's lips quivered and I knew she was about to start crying. So I kissed her lips, trying to help calm her down.

"Aww, see," the doc said, breaking the spell. "You two will be fine. But seriously, get some counseling before the baby comes. A newborn will test even the strongest of relationships."

I think we'll be just fine.

14

ALEXA

Just before walking into my parents' home only two days after we had the official pregnancy news confirmed by the doctor, I felt like I might throw up. "Hold on. I'm feeling a little sick."

Patton put his arm around me, holding me against his side. "Lean on me, Alexa. I don't want you falling down."

The door opened and there stood my father. "You didn't ring the bell?"

Swallowing hard, I knew it was nerves that had upset my stomach. "We're here."

Patton chuckled. "It's nice to see you again, Mr. De La Cruz."

"Mr. De La Cruz?" He slapped Patton on the shoulder as we came inside. "You call me Dad."

I looked at my father with a gaping mouth. "Are you sure?"

"Of course, I'm sure." He held out his arm, gesturing for us to sit down. "And call my wife Mamma. She'll love that."

Patton nodded but looked at me out of the corner of his eye. I knew that would make him uncomfortable. He was already having to lie to people he respected, and now this? It was too much, and I knew that. But telling my parents that Patton shouldn't call them that would raise red flags.

Mom came into the room with a photo album in her hands. "You're here. Good. I've just put the finishing touches on this."

Patton and I sat next to each other on the sofa, and my mother approached to place the album on my lap. I held my breath when I saw the words she'd written in gold ink across the cover. "Mr. and Mrs. Patton Nash." I wanted to cry; it was so sweet of her to do. "Mamma, you shouldn't have."

She took a seat in her favorite chair and my father took the one next to hers. "Not commemorate my angel's marriage? Are you crazy? Go ahead, look inside."

I didn't want to look through all the pictures Patton had taken of our fake wedding and honeymoon. But I knew my mother wouldn't have it any other way. So, I opened the book and found the very first picture of us as a married couple, kissing in front of the Elvis impersonator who had just finished the ceremony.

Patton ran his hand over the image. "Ah, there's my wife." He looked at me with what I swore was love in his blue eyes. "The day you made me the happiest man in the entire world." His lips pressed against my cheek and I felt like the air had left my lungs.

Oh yeah, he's putting on a show for my parents.

Taking a deep breath to get oxygen back to my brain, I played my part as a loving wife. "And you've made each day after that one the happiest days of my life, mi amor." I kissed his cheek and felt the warmth of his skin beneath my lips. It made my blood run hot, my juices begin to flow inside of me.

"You two look so in love," my mother gushed.

Instead of taking a painful trip down fake-memory lane, Patton saved us the trouble by closing the album then placing it on the coffee table in front of us. "Thank you so much for this," he paused, "Mamma."

My mother put her hand to her heart as tears made her eyes shimmer. "Oh, my son—my son, you are so welcome."

"Your daughter and I have some amazing news for you two," Patton let them know.

My father sat up, taking notice. "News?" He reached over, taking my mother's hand. "Tell us."

I looked at Patton, who nodded at me. "Okay. I'll tell you the news then." I couldn't believe how happy they both looked as they anticipated what I had to say. Their reaction would be so different from what I'd thought it would be when I first took the pregnancy test. My heart sped up as I shouted, "We're pregnant!"

My parents jumped up, hugging each other, then turned to us as Patton and I stood. Before I knew it, we were in a family hug, with me and Patton sandwiched between them.

Overjoyed with how they took the news, I could only look at my husband—the man who'd made all this possible. "Thank you." I took his face between my hands. "Thank you for making me your wife and giving me the chance to be a mother."

His eyes searched mine and I couldn't believe how much emotion I saw in them. "Thank you for becoming my wife and making me a father. I adore you." He kissed my lips softly. "I love you, my sweet wife."

My heart stopped. He'd never said that to me before. *Does he really mean it?*

Before I could say anything, my mother pulled me away from Patton. "You will stay the night here. We will make a wonderful meal and invite the family over to hear your good news. Your brother will be overcome with joy, I can tell you that right now."

Looking over my shoulder at Patton who gazed at me, I knew he was the only reason my news was being taken in this positive way. "I love you," I shouted back to him. "More than you will ever know."

His smile made my heart feel as if it bled inside my chest. I wanted this to be real so badly that I didn't know what to do. I had to make him fall in love with me, the way I'd fallen in love with him.

It had been so easy to fall for the man. He was perfect and wonderful. Thoughtful, kind, considerate, and above all of that, he was as selfless as anyone could be.

But it's all fake.

"Come, I will teach you how to make empanadas, my angel. That way you can make them for my grandchildren. I know you two will make the most gorgeous grandchildren for me and your father. And we will adore each and every one of them." She pulled a bowl out from under the cabinet. "I wonder if God will give you more children than he gave me." She giggled like a little girl. "I hope so. I want so many of them that I can spoil rotten."

"You don't know how happy it makes me to see you happy about this baby, Mamma." I wasn't lying about that. Taking her hands, I looked into her eyes, eyes that I hoped I would get to look into for many more years to come. "I love you."

"And I love you." She kissed my cheek. "Now, come. Let us make a feast for our family, so you can tell them all the good news."

My father and Patton joined us in the kitchen. Patton came up behind me, wrapping his arms around me and resting his hands on my stomach. "Should I go start up the barbeque pit? I overheard you two talking about a feast to celebrate our happy news."

I ran my hand along his firm jaw, loving the way it felt to be held by him. "That would be nice, mi amor. Some juicy ribs sound yummy to me."

"I'll go to the store to get the meat," my father said. "There's wood and charcoal in the shed in back, son. You know where everything is. Get the fire going, and by the time I get back we can season it all up and get it cooking."

"It feels good to be back home," Patton said then kissed the top of my head before letting me go. "I'll be out back if you need me, babe."

I spotted some fresh lemons. "I'll make some lemonade and bring it out to you soon."

His dark brows raised as he licked his lips before disappearing out the backdoor. My mother's hand on my shoulder took me out of the daze I'd been in since he first wrapped his arms around me. "You two are lucky to have found such a great love."

"I think so too." It wasn't exactly a lie. I thought we did have something growing between us. I felt a bond with Patton. I wasn't sure if it came from knowing him my whole life or what he was doing for me, but I felt a connection that held us together.

Before I knew it, my extended family filled the house and the backyard. Everyone congratulated us on the marriage and the baby. I had to show several of my cousins the photo album my mother had made for us. And looking at those pictures made something click inside of me.

This can't be fake.

Patton had to have feelings for me. And I knew I had them for him.

The night was long, but eventually everyone left and it was time to get to bed. Mamma led us down the hallway. "I've redone your old bedroom, Alexa. Since you have your own home now, I know you're never coming back to live here. So, all the pink is gone, and this is a guest room now."

She opened the door and I saw that my twin bed was gone. A large bed sat in its place, and curtains blew in the breeze. The cool air swirled around me, drawing me into the room. "Goodnight. I'll see you in the morning. We'll go down to Georgie's for breakfast tacos and coffee."

Patton took my hand, leading me into the room. "Sounds good, Mamma."

She closed the door, leaving us alone as I looked at the bed. There wasn't any other furniture in the room. "Looks like we're going to have to sleep together tonight." I wasn't the least bit sorry about that. We'd each brought one overnight bag with a change of clothes in it, but we'd planned on staying at a hotel, in two different rooms. I'd gotten used to sleeping in the nude, as I didn't like the constriction of clothing while I slept. I didn't know how Patton slept.

"I'll sleep on top of the blanket and you can sleep underneath it." He turned his back to me and began taking off his shirt.

I couldn't stop staring at him as he undressed. His muscles made magnificent shadows on his body as the light from the lamp hit him in all the right ways. "I hope my family wasn't too much for you today." A lot of them had joined us, and we weren't exactly a quiet bunch. It might've been overwhelming at times for him—not that he'd ever shown it.

He turned to face me, his abs making it hard for me to look him in the eyes, but I didn't want to get caught checking him out. "Alexa, I know all of them. I have been around your family for many years. You should know by now that nothing about you or your family is too much for me."

Fingering the top button of my shirt, I nodded. "Yeah." My mouth watered, begging to taste him in ways I'd only dreamed of. "You know, if it's going to be too hard for you to sleep with me, I can make a pallet on the floor."

"Like I'd let you do that." He chuckled, the sound deep and probably a lot sexier than he'd meant it to sound. "And I don't want to sleep on a cold, hard floor either. It'll be fine."

Unbuttoning my shirt, I thought he should know what he was up against. "I thought we'd be staying in a hotel. I've been sleeping without anything on for the last couple of months. And I didn't bring anything to sleep in. So, I'll just be in my bra and panties."

He dropped his jeans, stepped out of them, then laid on top of the blanket, wearing only tight boxer briefs that left nothing to the imagination. "I won't look, if that's what you're afraid of. I am, above all else, a gentleman."

My heart broke a little at that. If he found it so easy to ignore me while I was literally half naked in front of him, then he must not be attracted to me at all.

With a silent sigh, I started getting ready for bed.

15

PATTON

I would never make the first move—not ever. It wouldn't be right to do that to someone in Alexa's situation.

She'd called me her angel. She'd called me her hero. Heroes and angels didn't put the moves on the people who adored them. When you added in everything I'd done for her lately—knowing how grateful she felt for it all, it just wouldn't have been right for me to let her know that I wanted her. And I wanted her in the worst way.

Lying on top of that blanket as she undressed down to her bra and panties, I knew I should stop looking at her. They matched, too. A perfect little set made of pink satin, a tiny bow at her cleavage and one in the middle of the top of her panties.

Her body was smoking hot. Round hips, thick thighs, a midsection that dipped in all the right places, and then her heavy breasts. Breasts that would only get heavier as the pregnancy went on.

I turned to my side, not wanting her to see me checking her out. "Do you know if there's like a throw blanket or something in here? It's a little on the cool side." I needed to hide the boner that was welling up inside my underwear.

"Knowing my mother, I bet there is one at the top of the closet." She went over to the closet and I snuck a peek, taking in that luscious ass of hers. Perky, bouncy, and plump. She had no idea just how appealing she really was.

I watched her move up on her tippy toes, stretching her body as she reached up for the blanket. I should've gotten up to help her. But if I had, then she would've seen what she'd done to me. I couldn't do that to her. "It's okay if you can't reach it."

Wiggling her fingers, she finally got it and pulled it down. It fell right into her arms and she brought it back to me. "No, I'm not about to let you get cold."

There are other ways to make sure I stay nice and warm, honey.

She laid the blanket out to cover me as I lay on my side, hiding the effect she had on me. I knew I shouldn't even be thinking about the what if's, but I couldn't stop myself.

What if she made the first move? What if she told me she really loved me? What if she asked me to make her my wife in every way?

Closing my eyes, I knew I'd drunk one or two too many beers. Her brother and cousins had kept making sure I had a cold one in my hand all night long. I knew why her cousins had. They had no idea the ruse behind the marriage and baby. But Luci? Why he hadn't thought about how hard it would be for me to keep my hands off his sister when we went to bed together, I did not know.

Of course he wouldn't know, you idiot. He trusts you to keep your distance.

Every time I turned around, there she was, looking cute, sweet, and gorgeous. So, naturally I thought we should put on a good show. I'd grab her up, kiss her, hug her, tell her how happy she'd made me and how much I loved her.

She thought it was all for show though. What if she knew none of it was fake?

The bed moved as she got under the blanket. "Well, you have

a good sleep then, Patton."

I hated this—absolutely hated it. "Yeah, you too."

All day and night we'd pawed at each other like lust-filled teenagers. And here we were, in bed together, acting like none of that had even happened.

But that's the way it had to be. And I thought that's the way she wanted it. There were so many things I wanted to know. Like if she felt anything romantic for me. I wanted to know if she ever thought about us making this marriage into a real one and making a lifelong commitment to each other as well as to our baby.

Our baby.

One by one, my brothers had come to me, wanting to give me their advice. And I listened to them all. But I didn't agree with any of them.

They all agreed that this was a bad idea. They all agreed that this would end badly. They even all agreed that it would be Alexa who would be hurt the worst in this thing.

None of them knew about how I felt though. I hadn't admitted it to anyone. I barely let myself think about it.

I loved her. I adored her. And I already loved the baby we would raise together.

Doesn't that make this all real?

As soon as she turned out the lamp, I turned over to look at her in the moonlight. I knew it would bring out her beauty even more. The silver rays ran through her dark hair, making me think about the future, when she would be older and have silver streaks in her hair. And where I would be when that happened? "Do you think about the future, Alexa?"

"All the time." Lacing her fingers, she rested her hands on her chest. "But who doesn't?"

I knew it wasn't the right thing to do, but I did it anyway, laying my hand on her stomach. "Do you want a boy or a girl?"

"I want a healthy baby. I'll be just as in love with a boy as I will be a girl." She turned her head to look at me. The full moon reflected in her dark eyes. "And what do you want?"

"Same." I didn't care what sex it was, just as long as it was healthy. "Do you think you'll want to have more kids after this one?"

"Probably." She smiled at me. "I hope you have some of your own someday too."

I hated that everyone but me thought of this baby as someone else's. Not knowing what to say about that, I pulled my hand off her and turned over. "Night."

Her hand on my shoulder made my heart ache and my cock pulse. "Patton, I've upset you. I'm sorry that I say the wrong thing sometimes. It's just that I feel bad about you doing all of this for me and this baby. This is all my fault. Yet you're the one who's taking on the responsibility of my actions. I feel bad about it. And I don't know how things will turn out for us. It's nice to think that we can raise this child together, even once we go our separate ways. But the honest truth is that many people who divorce have a hard time raising a child properly."

Then let's not divorce.

I held my breath as so many emotions bottled up inside of me. I wanted to talk to Luciano and ask him how he'd feel if I was honest with Alexa about my feelings. And if she wasn't into me the way I was into her, then I would respect that, of course. I wouldn't ever bring it up again. But I desperately wanted to know if she felt the way I did.

"Yeah, you're right." I didn't want to talk about things ending with us. I loved having her around. I loved her company—more than I'd ever enjoyed anyone else's. "I guess we should just get some sleep. We'll have breakfast with your parents—maybe Luci will join us. After that, we should head back to Austin. I've got a meeting with my cousins at their ranch in Carthage on Monday.

They want to know how their investment—the resort—is doing. It's an early one and I'll have to head out around five on Monday morning. I don't want to get in late tomorrow night or anything."

"I understand." Her hand slid off my shoulder. "Night."

I'd wanted to improve the communication between us. But it seemed impossible. I couldn't say what I wanted to. I couldn't put her in the position of having to accept or reject me.

It wouldn't be fair or right. Plus, I would never know if she accepted me for me or if she simply felt a sense of gratitude or even guilt. I was fairly certain that she wouldn't reject me. She was too kind to do that to someone who had done so much for her.

Only then did I begin to realize that being a good person wasn't always easy. And when one added alcohol to the situation, it made it that much harder.

I'd signed up for this. I'd known what I was getting into. Or I had thought I had, anyway.

I had never planned to end up falling for her. I'd had no idea I would end up falling in love with that tiny whooshing heartbeat, but I had. I'd fallen in love with the idea of us—as a family.

That was my mistake—no one else's. I'd let my feelings run away with me. But I could pull them back, tie them up, hide them away.

When we were back home, we wouldn't have to touch, hug, kiss the way we had to do when we were around her parents. I suddenly felt a twinge of empathy for actors. How were they able to turn it off and on like that? It was a mystery to me.

Wait. Actors are constantly changing lovers. Maybe I should've done some research on that before I went and took on this whole thing.

Maybe the mere act of holding someone long enough was all it took to make you feel connected to them in a special way. Maybe kissing someone, even when no feelings were involved in the first place, eventually led to feelings. Maybe just being around the same person, day in and day out, led to stronger connections.

I turned over to look at Alexa. Her eyes were closed but she wasn't breathing deeply enough to be sleeping.

"Alexa?" I whispered.

She kept her eyes closed. "Yes?"

"Do you think that acting like we're in love will ever make us think that we really are?" I held my breath, hoping like hell she would open her eyes, look at me, and tell me that she loved me —for real.

"You've had too much to drink."

"Yeah, I know. But what about the question? Do you think all this acting might affect us?" I didn't want her to think the alcohol was making me ask this question. Sure, it might've been, but so what?

"I think we have always had love for each other in one form or another. You're very close with my family, and that means you're very close with me. I also feel close to you. But the kind of love between a husband and a wife isn't something that can be faked into being real."

She turned her head and her eyes opened. "We wouldn't be human if touching like we've done tonight didn't arouse us. But neither of us wants to hurt the other. We're not in love. Not that way. And I don't want you to worry about me. I know that's what you're doing, you know. You are worrying that I'm so young and naïve, and that I'll think that all the attention you've been paying to me today will make me think we're in love. But you don't need to worry about that."

She couldn't have been more wrong. "Glad we're on the same page. Goodnight then."

"Goodnight." She turned over, putting her back to me.

And I closed my eyes, feeling the backs of them sting with tears I wouldn't allow to fall. *I shouldn't have drunk so much.*

16

ALEXA

Going from one client to another, I was walking down the hallway at the spa when I saw Patton coming my way.

"Hey," he called out. "I just got a phone call from our OB-GYN's office. They said they couldn't get a hold of you, but they had to reschedule our three-month check-up appointment. It'll be Monday of next week, instead of tomorrow."

My back ached and I put my hand on it, stretching to see if it would ease up a bit. "That's a relief. I wasn't looking forward to another exam anyway." I shuddered as I recalled the last one and how completely uncomfortable it had been.

Taking my hand, he tugged me along with him. "You need a break, little mama. I bet you haven't eaten a thing since breakfast."

"I had a candy bar around noon. One of the other massage therapists didn't come in, so my workload doubled—I've had back-to-back clients all day. And I've got the backache to show for it."

"I wish you would've told me that sooner." He shook his head. "No, I don't mean that. It isn't your job to tell me those kinds of things. It is Hailey's, though. I can make a call and get someone to fill in for the missing therapist."

My back wasn't letting me catch a break. I wasn't one to whine about being in any discomfort, but I had more than just myself to think about. "Can you see if you can get two people to come fill in? My back is killing me. I think I need to get off my feet for a while."

He pulled me into his office and made me sit on the sofa. "You lay down. Get those feet up. I'll handle that right now."

"I've got a client waiting," I whimpered as I laid back. "I can't just let that poor lady wait until someone can get here to replace me. I'll just rest for a minute then go take care of her. The replacement can take the next one."

"You'll stay right where you are and not worry about that. I'll make sure Hailey knows what I'm doing." He kissed me on the forehead. "You're lucky that your husband is one of the bosses around here."

"I am lucky for that." I felt lucky that Patton was my husband for so many reasons—work was just the tip of the iceberg.

Trying to relax, I closed my eyes, but the pain in my back wasn't going away. My stomach began to hurt too, so I got up, much to Patton's disapproval. "What? What is it? You need to lie down. I can get you whatever you need."

"I need to go to the bathroom." I knew he couldn't do that for me. "I'll be right back. My stomach just started feeling kind of icky."

"Back pain and now stomach pain?" His expression told me he didn't like what he was hearing. "I'm going to call the doctor's office back to ask about that."

"I'm sure it's just that I've been so busy today. Once I can really rest, I'll be fine." I headed out to go to the nearest ladies' restroom as my stomach began cramping.

Getting to the toilet suddenly became an emergency as the

cramps just kept getting worse and worse. *I shouldn't have eaten that candy bar!*

I thought it was a simple stomachache, but when I pulled my pants down, I found something I wasn't supposed to find. *Blood!*

Moving like lightning, I yanked my pants back up then went out the door. Patton was there, waiting for me. "The nurse said to bring you in right now."

"I don't want to go to the doctor's office." I felt like I might faint all of a sudden and fell back against the wall. "I need to go to the emergency room. I'm bleeding."

Before I knew it, I was in Patton's arms and he was rushing to his truck and then to the nearest hospital. "Just stay calm, honey. No need to panic."

"What if the baby is in danger, Patton? I feel very panicky." Taking deep breaths, I tried to calm myself. I knew feeling stressed out wasn't good for the baby. "I'm only three months into the pregnancy—too many bad things can happen this early on." I closed my eyes, praying that this baby wouldn't be taken away from me.

Sure, it had a loser for a biological father. But the father it was going to have would be an amazing one. I would be an amazing mother, too. We'd be there for this child, if it could just hang on.

Patton scooped me up, carrying me into the emergency room of the South Austin Medical Center. As soon as the glass doors slid open, he shouted, "We've got a possible miscarriage here and need help now! Right now!"

The double stainless-steel doors opened as if his words alone controlled them. A man wearing blue scrubs waved us in. "Come on back."

Moving like the wind, Patton took me to the bed the man pointed at. "Everything's going to be okay, baby. You're here now and they will make sure of it."

The man nodded at me with a smile on his face. "I'm Davin. Now, tell me what's going on here." He pulled out a clipboard that hung at the end of the bed, handing it to Patton. "I'm assuming you're the father."

"I am." Patton took the clipboard. "You want me to fill this out?"

"I would appreciate it, yes." Davin turned his attention back to me. "So, how far along are you, Ms.—Mrs.—?"

"Mrs. Nash. Alexa. And I'm three months pregnant."

"Okay," he said with a calm tone. "So, what has you coming here today, instead of going to your doctor? I am assuming you have seen one for the pregnancy?"

I nodded my head. "I've been seeing Doctor Barclay," I told him as I tried not to cry. "My back has been hurting for about two and a half hours. My stomach began cramping about a half hour ago. And when I went to the bathroom, there was blood on my panties. I didn't want to risk the longer drive to her office."

"How much blood?" he asked.

Patton stopped filling out the paperwork to look at me, waiting to see what my answer was. I could see the fear in his eyes and knew he really did care about this baby that I carried— a baby that wasn't even his. He cared deeply for it.

"Not a lot. But with everything else I'm feeling, it concerned me."

Pulling the curtain around to give us some privacy, the nurse then went to a drawer, pulled out a hospital gown and laid it at the foot of the bed. "Okay, you put this on and the doctor will come do an examination shortly to see what's going on. Take everything off," he said as he looked over his shoulder. "Everything."

"Okay." I felt the frown form on my face. "Ugh."

Patton put the clipboard down as I stood up to undress. "Let me help you."

"I've got to get completely naked, Patton." I wasn't going to let him see me stark naked.

Cocking his head, he gave me a no-nonsense look. "Do you think that you'll be wearing much more than that when you have this baby in a few months, Alexa?"

"I haven't really thought about that." Mostly because it scared the crap out of me.

"Let me help you." He picked up the gown, unfurling it in front of me. "Take your clothes off. This will cover you up, and I swear I won't look. This thing ties in the back. I don't think you can manage that."

Along with the physical pain came the pain of embarrassment as I took every stitch of clothing off, kicking my bloody panties under my pants to hide them. "This is not what I expected to be doing today."

"Me neither, but here we are." He held out the gown as I put my arms through the sleeves. "Turn around and I'll tie it."

I felt the cold air on my exposed bottom and knew he was going to see it as soon as I turned around. "God, this is horrible."

"I'm not looking." His fingers grazed my skin as he tied the gown closed. "There. Now lay back down."

As I lay down, he leaned over, scooping up my clothes. "Uh, I should do that."

"You're not getting back out of that bed until they say you can." He rolled the clothes into a neat ball then shoved them into a plastic bag that he found on the counter. "I'm going to tell my assistant to go to our place to bring some fresh clothes for you to put on when it's time for us to leave." He took out his cell and typed in the message.

"You think of everything." I watched him until he was done and put the phone away to look at me. "Thank you."

"It's my pleasure." Coming to me, he put his hand on my

stomach. "Hey, you in there. You've got a mommy and daddy out here who love you very much, so hang on in there. Please."

Moving my hand over his, I felt the tears dripping down my cheeks. "You really are a daddy."

He leaned over, kissed my stomach then whispered, "I *am* your daddy."

The curtain opened and a man in a white coat came in, closing the curtain behind him. "I'm Doctor Flanigan. I've been caught up on your situation and feel fairly certain about what the diagnosis will be, but I'll have to do an exam."

Patton came to stand beside me, taking my hand in his. "I hope it's not too bad."

"We'll have to see." With no sheet to cover me at all, he unceremoniously pulled up the gown, bent my knees then moved to the end of the bed, pulling a big light up behind him before putting on one glove. "There's not much leakage at this time."

I gasped as he plunged an ultrasound wand into me. I heard a low growl come from Patton. "Hey, man. Ease up there. You can be a hell of a lot gentler than you're being with her."

"So, you're one of those kinds of husbands, huh?" He nodded. "Okay. Well, I need to switch to an abdominal ultrasound now anyways." He suited his action to his words as I tried not to panic. "You can expect more bleeding as a side effect of the exam. But that should stop by tomorrow," He explained as he now pushed the probe against my skin.

"So, the exam put the baby in further danger?" I could tell Patton was seeing red as he asked the question.

"No. Not at all," the doctor tried to explain, as he could see the steam coming from Patton's ears. "The bleeding will be from the vaginal walls, this time," he looked away from Patton and back to me. "It looks like you're experiencing something called a subchorionic hematoma. This means there is some blood gathering under the placenta. This is fairly common, and is not likely to cause any complications with your pregnancy." He let out a huge sigh of relief at this news.

"This usually resolves itself, and the baby's heartbeat is still strong. You'll need to see your regular doctor within a week to check on it, but until then, stay off your feet and no hanky-panky."

"So, that's it then?" Patton asked, looking as relieved as I felt.

"That is it." He pulled the curtain back. "She can get dressed, and as soon as the nurse brings you the discharge papers, you are free to go."

I looked at Patton with a dazed stare, feeling overwhelmed at how quickly everything had happened. "So, the baby's okay?"

"It sounds like it. But you're not going back to work until our doctor says you can. Until our appointment next week, you'll be my patient at home." He looked down at his phone and started texting—I assumed to ask his assistant if she was close by with the clean clothes.

"You don't have to stay at home with me, Patton. I'm sure I'll be fine while you work." I sat up, putting my legs over the side of the bed.

"I *will* stay at home with you. I'm *not* leaving you alone."

17

PATTON

The doorbell rang. "That must be Doctor Barclay now."

After the follow-up appointment with our regular doctor, Alexa had been told to stay home and off her feet as much as possible. That meant the doc had to make house calls, and had been doing so for the last few months. I opened the door, welcoming her in. "Afternoon, doc. The little lady is on the sofa."

"Afternoon, Patton." She came in and walked straight to the living room. "So, this is the sixth-month checkup, and I am going to need you to take her in for a sonogram later this week. As long as there's been no more bleeding." The hematoma hadn't yet reabsorbed into the placenta as the doctors had hoped, so we were being very careful about monitoring Alexa.

"She's done really well this month. I don't think we'll have a problem taking her in for that." I went to stand next to Alexa as she sat on the sofa. "You ready?"

Nodding, she smiled at the doctor. "I've been doing well this last month. No bleeding at all, and only a little cramping."

"And how about staying off your feet?" She pulled a stethoscope from her bag.

"I've been doing pretty good with that. Only walking to the kitchen now and then when I don't know exactly what I want to eat and have to stare into the fridge to make up my mind." She laughed as she looked up at me. "Other than that, Patton has made sure I don't need to get up for much at all."

"Good to hear." The doctor listened to Alexa's heart then her lungs, then checked all her other vitals before listening to her tummy. "Sounds good here. A steady heartbeat is always good to hear. So, what's it going to be with the sonogram? Do you want to know the sex of the baby, or is it going to be a surprise?"

Alexa and I had been waiting on getting the nursery painted until we knew if we were having a boy or a girl. "We do want to know what we're having."

"Great. I'll put that in the notes." She put away her things then asked, "Any questions for me, Alexa?"

"I'd like to know if you think I'll carry the baby to full term." She'd been having bad dreams about the baby coming early. In the dreams, it was always covered in blood and screaming, she told me, and it was tiny as could be.

"I understand why you might be worried about that. Now that you're twenty-four weeks, the baby has developed its lungs and vital organs. Now, of course, this doesn't mean that these organs are fully developed, so the baby would need to be in the NICU if you were to deliver it any time soon. Each week that you go without delivering a preterm baby from here on out is even better. So, don't be in a hurry to have this baby. The longer it bakes in your oven, the better."

"So, if I had this baby right now, it would survive?" Alexa asked, looking relieved.

"I didn't say that," the doctor let her know. "There are no guarantees. Not even with a baby that is born at full term. I'm sorry to have to say that to you, and I know it's never easy for a mother to hear. But it has to be said. That little baby inside of you needs you to take the best care of yourself that you possibly can. But sometimes, that doesn't change what happens in the delivery room. I don't want you to dwell on that. Please, don't. Focus on having a healthy baby. If, for some reason, you do have the baby early, every week you can keep it inside of you gives it that much of a higher survival rate."

Though I knew she was just trying to keep us informed, I didn't like what I was hearing at all. I didn't think Alexa did either when all she said was a soft, "Oh."

I ran my hand over her head. "Don't think about that, babe. Everything will be fine. You'll see."

Alexa took my hand, holding it to her heart. "Feel that?"

It was beating like crazy. "Calm down. Everything is going to be fine."

The doctor headed for the door. "I'm optimistic that the hematoma has finally cleared itself, so get your check-up and that sonogram done within the week and they'll send it to me. I'll discuss it with you over a video call later that same day."

I went to show her out. As I opened the door, I found Luciano standing there, about to press the doorbell. "Well, hello," he said to the doctor, taking her hand then kissing the top of it instead of shaking it.

"Um," the doctor muttered as she looked at me. "A friend of yours, Patton?"

"Our baby's uncle," I told her. "Alexa's brother."

Luciano let go of her hand. "Luciano De La Cruz, Doctor Barclay. It's a pleasure to meet the lady who has been keeping my sister healthy."

"Thanks." She stepped back to let him come in. "I was just on my way out."

Luciano came inside, eyeing the woman. "You're rather young to be a doctor, aren't you?"

"Last I checked thirty wasn't that young." She smiled at him.

"But flattery will get you everywhere." She walked out the door, shaking her head as she went.

After closing the door, I had to laugh. "Do you ever meet a woman that you don't hit on?"

"Once in a while. But not often, no." He joined his sister in the living room. "And how are we doing today, my little princesa?"

"I'm doing okay, I guess. I mean, the doctor just started talking about what would happen if the baby's premature. It sort of frightened me." She let out a long, sad sigh.

I took the place next to her, taking her hand in mine. "Don't let that upset you. You and I both know that we're doing everything we can to make sure this baby is going to be healthy and happy. And that's all we can do."

She leaned her head on my shoulder. "Yes, that is all we can do."

Luci looked at me with a weird expression. "I'm going to grab myself a beer. Want one while I'm up, Patton?"

"Nah." I jerked my head at the glasses on the coffee table. "We're drinking some herbal tea."

Alexa patted my hand. "Patton likes to eat and drink healthy with me. He's incredibly supportive."

"Yeah, I can see that." He walked to the bar, going behind it to get a cold beer from the built-in mini fridge.

He hadn't been over for the last couple of months, and he seemed to be a bit confused about the way Alexa and I were getting along. We'd been together every day, all day long. And we both had a fair amount of concern for the baby. That had given us something to bond over. And I supposed it showed.

Not wanting to make Luci feel uncomfortable, I got up. "I'm going to go see what we can make for dinner tonight since we have a guest."

"I don't want you to go to any trouble for me, Patton," Luci said as he came to sit down with the fresh beer in his hand. "Whatever you have on hand will work just fine for me."

I wanted to give the two of them some time alone to talk. "Okay, I won't go out of my way or anything then."

Going to the fridge, I opened the freezer to find some steaks, chicken, and sausages in there. Pulling out the chicken, I put it in the sink then went to see what else I could find to go with it.

I loved making healthy meals for Alexa and the baby. I'd always cooked for myself, but never for anyone else. It turned out that I loved cooking for her.

Maybe it was because she was always so pleased by everything that I made for her. She would gush about it, no matter what it was. And she would always thank me for making it for her.

Alexa was just about the most grateful person I'd ever known. She thanked me for the smallest things. It was just one more thing that I had come to adore about her.

That I'd come to love about her.

I loved her and knew that with a certainty I'd never had before. But I wasn't sure she shared the same feelings for me. Not that it mattered all that much just then. Sex was off the table anyway, what with the problems with her pregnancy. But it would matter later, after the baby came and we had to decide if we were going to stay together or stick with the plan of breaking up.

I couldn't see my life without her in it. And once the baby came, I knew both of them would become my life. I didn't want it any other way.

Leaning over, I opened the vegetable bin inside the fridge and pulled out some carrots and broccoli. When I stood up to put them on the counter, I found Luciano coming into the kitchen with a grim expression on his face.

I wasn't sure what to say to him. I figured he wasn't happy

about how I was practically all over his sister. So, I tried to steer clear of that conversation. "So, stir fry chicken sound good to you? I've got fresh carrots and broccoli. I think I've got fettuccini I can make too. That sounds healthy, right?"

"Sure." He leaned back against the island bar.

The vibes he gave off were so strong that I could practically see waves rolling off him. It wasn't anger. It was something else that I couldn't quite put my finger on it. And I didn't want to talk about it either. "You can help me cook if you want." I slid a cutting board to him then a knife and the veggies. "Care to cut these up while I defrost the chicken?"

"Sure." He took the knife in his hand then looked at me with wide eyes. He looked a little on the crazy side.

Immediately, I knew giving him a knife was a bad idea. "Or you can defrost the chicken and I'll cut up the veggies." I wasn't going to move any closer to him than I had to. "Here you go." I held out the package of frozen chicken. "Just slide those things over here and you can put this into the microwave behind you. That makes more sense, anyway, doesn't it?"

He held onto the knife, his eyes glazing over as he stood there with his mouth slightly ajar. He moved his mouth a few times before any words came out of it, "She's in love with you."

"I'm sorry." I couldn't have heard him right. "She's what?"

"My sister is in love with you, Patton. I can see it in her eyes. It's not only that she adores you; she isn't just smitten with you. She is in love with you—heart and soul."

I froze. I had no idea what to say to him. Not because I was worried about what he would think or say back to me. I was frozen because I hadn't seen the things he'd seen in her eyes. I hadn't seen the love he spoke of.

Have I been blind all this time? Is Alexa really in love with me?

18

ALEXA

The curtains blew in the cool breeze as I lay in my bed tossing and turning—wanting. I threw the blanket to the floor, I'd had enough of it wrapping around my body, constricting me, holding me prisoner. I yearned to be free.

The door moved and my eyes darted over to it. I watched as a shadowy figure moved into my bedroom. I stayed still, not sure if I should act as if I was asleep or not.

As the figure moved closer to my bed, it became clear by the broad shoulders exactly who had come to visit in the night. But what he'd come for I had yet to determine.

Perhaps he'd only come to my bedside to check on me, to make sure everything was okay. Or maybe he'd also grown tired of waiting for what was rightfully his for the taking.

Me.

For the longest time, the figure loomed at the foot of my bed. Frozen, I was excited, hopeful, and wanted him to come to me the way a husband comes to his wife.

Slowly, warm fingers moved along the bottom of my foot, inciting a riot of butterflies in my stomach, along with spreading fire through my entire body. *Yes, finally.*

Moving one knee onto the bed, he gently pushed my legs apart so he could get between them. His lips grazed along my inner thigh as his hands moved up each leg.

Still, I couldn't seem to move. I didn't want him to stop what he was doing or ask me if it was okay. It was more than okay—it was exactly what I wanted. And I didn't want to discuss it; I just wanted it to happen already.

I couldn't breathe as his mouth moved up to kiss my intimate lips. Softly, he kissed then blew warm breath over me, sending chills along my spine. A flick of his tongue barely touched my pearl, which had already swollen for him.

Kissing it, he flicked his tongue over it as his hands moved around to my butt, lifting me up to give him better access to my sweet spot. As his intimate kiss went deeper, it forced a low moan out of me to which he moaned back, the vibration sending me into depths of ecstasy I hadn't known existed.

My fingers curled into the sheet underneath me; I pulled so hard the fitted sheet came off the bed corners above me. My feet moved back and forth as my body went insane with what he was doing to me.

He'd never kissed my mouth like this. Never used his tongue in the way he was kissing me now. Our kisses had been on the chaste side. I liked this side better—much better.

A gentle sucking action on my pulsing pearl sent me over the edge. Something flashed through my body, sending fluids gushing down my canal. He moved his mouth, stabbing his tongue into me, drinking up what he'd made my body give him.

My canal pulsed around his tongue, wanting more than that from him. Pulling my knees up, I urged him to give me more as I ran my hands through his hair. He took the hint and began kissing his way up my body until his mouth met mine.

His tongue swept into my mouth at the same time he penetrated me with his hard, long, and wide manhood. I screamed with the pain that came with being stretched to fit him. But his kiss muffled the sound and in no time at all, the screams turned to moans of pure pleasure.

Wrapping my legs around him, I never wanted to let him go. I wanted to feel him inside of me for the rest of my life. I never wanted him to let me go or stop making love to me.

We moved like waves on the ocean together, stroking each other's bodies, moving our hands over every inch of the other person. We caressed every surface that we could reach without letting our mouths part.

He moved his hands into my hair, pulling it a bit as he moved faster, plunging into me harder. I cried out with the intense heat that came with each new place he found and stretched inside of me. I loved it all. I loved the pain, the smell, the absolute decadence of the act.

It wasn't soft. It wasn't sweet. It was primal, and I knew it was supposed to be this way. A primal need we both shared. This is the way sex was intended to be.

Raw, gritty, and full of demands from each body. I wanted him inside of me, moving, rocking my body in a way I didn't even know could be done. And he needed to be connected to me, to be a part of my body. He needed to feel my tight canal squeeze his male member in a hard, hot, wet way. It held him tightly, unwilling to release him.

"More," I moaned. "I want more. Give me more."

Moving faster, he thrust into me, making the bed shake and the headboard bang against the wall with every single move he made. "I'll give you more. I'll give you all you can take and then I'll give you just a bit more."

Panting hard, I dug my nails into his back as I bit his shoulder. "Yes! More! Yes!"

My body exploded for him once again. He didn't stop

though. He kept going, growling through it all, begging me, "Don't stop coming. Keep it going. God, this is amazing!"

My body forged on, pulsing, throbbing as it urged him to keep giving me more of what he had to offer. I couldn't stop. I kept going for him, just the way he wanted me to. I would give the man anything and everything he ever asked of me. If he would just keep giving me this, I would give him the whole world.

My heart pounded, my body drenched in sweat, and my mouth dry from panting. Still, I didn't want to stop for even a moment to take a drink of water or try to catch my breath. "Don't stop! I want more! God, help me, I want more!"

Knock, knock, knock. "Alexa? Are you okay in there?"

My eyes flew open. The sheets were wrapped around me, making it impossible to move. My breathing was ragged, my body covered in sweat. And only then did I begin to realize it had all been a dream. "Damn," I whispered to myself. "I'm okay."

"Are you sure?" he asked through the door. "You were screaming and moaning like you were in pain. Can I come in?"

Yanking the sheets off of my body, I could smell the sex in the air as I'd obviously orgasmed while sleeping. I had never done anything like that before. I'd actually never had an orgasm in my life. On one hand, I was extremely happy about being able to achieve such a magnificent thing. On the other hand, I was sort of ashamed that I'd done that all on my own, somehow.

"I'd rather you not. I'm okay. I was just having a nightmare." It was anything but a nightmare, but I had no idea how to explain why I was screaming in my sleep and moaning as if I was in pain.

"Are you sure?" he asked, not seeming to believe me.

"Yeah, I'm sure." I got up, needing to go take a shower. "I'm going to be in the bathroom. You can go back to bed, Patton."

"I'll be up for a while if you want to come get some warm milk or something to help you sleep more soundly," he offered. "Or I can bring some to you."

"That's okay." I smiled at this thoughtfulness. He was just so there for me in every way. "Night, mi amor."

"Okay then, night, pumpkin. Have sweet dreams and no more bad ones." His footsteps moved away from the door.

Walking into the bathroom, I looked at my reflection in the mirror. My cheeks were red, my sweat-soaked hair clung to my face and my entire body shimmered with perspiration. But I liked it. I liked the way I looked after having an orgasm. "If it was that good when I was alone, and in a dream, then what will it be like with my handsome husband? And will I ever get to find that out?"

Starting the shower, I had to wonder if that would actually ever happen. I knew there was no way we'd have sex before the baby came, as the doctor had told us sex was off the table until six weeks after the birth of the baby. But what about after that? Would Patton ever want what I did—a marriage that was as real as it could get?

Before my brother had left earlier that evening, he'd spoken to me in private. I didn't like what he had said to me. He told me that he could see that I was falling in love with Patton, and that I knew better than to do that to myself. Patton would never betray their friendship by doing anything inappropriate with me.

I'd kept my mouth shut tightly. I hadn't realized my heart was showing so clearly. I hadn't meant for it to.

Finally, I promised him that I would try to reign in my feelings for my husband. To which he chastised me for calling Patton my husband, reminding me that he'd set this whole thing up and Patton was merely doing him and I a favor. A favor we shouldn't ever take for granted.

Before I'd fallen asleep, I'd been thinking a lot about what my brother had said. And I thought about what Patton himself had told me. He was doing us a favor, but he wanted this baby—even though it wasn't his. He wanted to take care of it and me. That didn't seem like a favor to me. It seemed like he wanted us, like he didn't see us as a burden at all.

Rinsing off my body, I ran my hands over my swollen belly. "You've got a real father. Not some deadbeat. I'm not going to ruin that for you by asking for more than that. I don't want you to worry. Your mommy will put away her silly feelings so that you can have a great home and a great father."

I didn't know how easy it would be to do that, but I had to try—for the baby's sake. I had to try to get past this raging sexual attraction I felt for Patton. Even if he did want to have sex with me, he'd never tell me so. He was the perfect gentleman, and his allegiance to my brother was apparently off the charts.

Turning off the shower, I toweled off then went to bed, finding the sheets damp. Taking them off the bed, I got a fresh set out of the linen closet in the bathroom, and then made the bed.

My dreams needed to calm down about Patton. If it wasn't going to happen in real life, I'd rather not live it in my dream life. It made my heart ache to know that I'd never get to feel him that way, inside of me, touching me, stroking me, making love to me.

Dreaming about that had only made things harder for me, as a woman. What woman didn't want to feel all those things in real life with a man she loved?

I loved Patton and I knew that without a doubt. And I knew he had love for me. But what kind of love? I really wasn't sure.

But I was sure of one thing. He would never betray my brother. And it didn't seem as though my brother was ever going to see me as a grown woman. It also looked like he didn't think Patton was the man for me either.

19

PATTON

Lying on the exam table, Alexa tried her best not to look nervous as the technician lathered up the instrument that he was about to use to find out how the baby was doing and what sex it was.

"I don't want you to get your hopes up that we'll find out the sex today. Sometimes these little guys can be very tricky and refuse to roll the right way for us to see. The main reason we're doing the ultrasound is to make sure this baby is hitting all the milestones, and to see how the placenta is doing. Doctor Barclay will be able to assess that from the sonogram."

"I just want to be able to not call our baby an it anymore," I said with a chuckle.

Alexa nodded then reached out for my hand. "I don't know why I'm so nervous, but I am."

Taking her hand, I held it and smiled at her. "This won't be bad at all."

"Not the procedure. I know that won't be bad," she said. "I'm just worried that something might be wrong with the baby."

The technician ran the instrument over her belly, looking at the screen of his computer. "We will soon find that out for you, Mrs. Nash."

Sucking in her breath, she looked at me with worried eyes. "Let's see what we're having. I hope the baby will work with us. I'd like to get to see the nursery done before we bring it home."

"Me too." Leaning over, I kissed her forehead. "I'm sure things are fine with the baby."

"The baby is looking good," the tech said. "The heart is doing what it's supposed to be doing. The lungs are functioning well too." He ran the probe up and down the middle of her stomach. "And see that backbone there?"

I could see it quite clearly. "I do see that. This is even more amazing than I thought it would be."

"It is amazing," Alexa agreed. "That looks like a good spine to me." Her tiny smile looked radiant to me.

"Yep," the tech agreed. "Everything looks great with the skeletal system and the organs. So, in that regard, you've got nothing to worry about. Now, let's see if we can get it to move around a bit so we can get a peek at what's between its legs." He pushed the instrument down hard and the baby shifted. "Ah ha! Do you see that, Daddy?"

"I see something," I said as I blinked a few times. "Is that a—"

Alexa finished for me, "A tiny penis?"

"It is," the tech let us know. "You're having a boy."

Alexa's eyes were wide as she looked at me. "I know just what his name will be now."

"You do?" I was surprised about that, because she hadn't said a word to me about names. "And what will his name be?"

"He's going to carry his father's name." She looked back at the screen, instead of at me.

My chest deflated at her words. I hadn't thought in a million years that she'd want to name the child, that I'd raise and call my own, after the piece of shit who actually fathered it. "Oh."

Looking back at me with furrowed brows, she asked, "You don't want that, Patton?"

"You can do whatever you want." I tried not to look so disappointed, but I was kind of devastated.

Everything I'd done for her and the baby had been out of love in one form or another. I wasn't sure how I would feel if I had to call our son Alejandro, or even Alex. But it was up to her to name it, I supposed.

"Well, my brother's name has to be put in there too. And I want my father represented as well," she added. "Patton James Luciano De La Cruz-Nash. Doesn't that sound like a strong name?"

She's naming him after me!

I couldn't help it—I leaned over and kissed her on the lips. "I agree one thousand percent."

"Good." Her eyes shimmered with unshed tears. "I want him to be like you in every way. You're a good man and I know you'll do your absolute best to raise our son to be a good man too."

"I will." The way she talked—it was like we'd be together forever. The part of the plan about getting a divorce after the birth of the baby hadn't been brought up by either of us in many months. Of course, Luciano was a different story.

He'd brought that up when he'd told me he thought Alexa was in love with me. And I hadn't said anything to contradict him. I hadn't said anything at all, really. I'd let him do all the talking.

I wasn't sure if he'd said anything to Alexa about his suspicions. If he had, she didn't say a thing to me about it. But I was sure she would be too embarrassed to bring it up to me anyway.

Later, as we drove home from the appointment, Alexa's

phone rang. "It's the doctor. She must've already seen the sonogram," she explained as she hit answer. "Hello, Doctor Barclay."

Alexa put the phone on speaker so I could hear too. "I've gotten the results of the sonogram and the baby looks great. There is still a small hematoma that I'm concerned about this far into the pregnancy. So, I am revising your orders some. I want you to stay off your feet. You can go back and forth to the bathroom, but that's about it," she let us know.

"Patton, I want you to get a chair for the shower, so she can sit to bathe. No baths in the bathtub, though. If there is any bleeding at all, any cramps, contractions, anything that is worrisome to you, I want you to call me directly. Don't go through the office. If, for some reason, you don't get a hold of me and I don't return your call within a half hour, I want you to go to the labor and delivery department at Saint David's and let them know what's happening. I'll advise them of your situation today, so they'll be prepared and know about your case already. I'll come by next Wednesday at noon. I'll be coming to see you each week, so be ready for me to do pelvic exams each visit. Can you do that for me?"

"We can," I said as I smiled at Alexa. "Not a problem at all. We've got this."

"Thank you, Doctor Barclay," Alexa said, but she looked grim. "See you next week. Bye."

Reaching over, I took her hand. I knew she wasn't happy with the results. "I know you think this part is going to be rough."

Tears fell in rivers down her cheeks, which had turned red. "This is just so scary, Patton."

"I know, baby. I know." My heart hurt for her. I had no idea what it meant to be in her shoes. The life of the baby inside of her relied on her body until it was ready to come out.

"How come no one ever tells you that this sort of thing can

happen?" she sobbed. "I don't know why I thought I would have it easy when my own mother had it so hard. I don't know why I let that man take my virginity. I don't know why I let him have sex with me four more times, when every time was just a disappointment. I just kept thinking that it had to get better than that, or no one would bother to do it—except for procreation purposes."

My blood boiled at the thought of that low-life fucker using someone like Alexa just for sex. "He isn't worth talking about, baby. He's a worthless piece of shit. I wish I could erase all that from your mind. I wish I could make this baby mine and not his."

She pulled our clasped hands to her heart as she cried. "This baby is yours. He will always be yours. Never doubt that. I will forget about that awful man. I swear to you that I will. I will never utter his name again. I will never whine about my stupidity. From now on, I will only think one thought about this child. He is yours. You are his father. That's the way it is and the way it will always be," I could hear the conviction ringing in her voice. She'd made a complete turnaround from where she'd begun.

Nodding, I couldn't help but wonder how much the boy would end up looking like the biological father. After all, they were both full-blooded Hispanics, and I was—well, I was just a Caucasian with some Irish and German in my blood.

What if people don't think he's my real son? What if Alexa's parents don't think I'm the real father?

I didn't say a word about my worries out loud. Alexa had enough on her mind without my fears getting into her head. And right now, she needed me to be strong—she needed me to be her rock.

"Let's just clam down. You know I'll be here every step of the way." I did mean that. I didn't ever want things to end. I wanted so much more with her. I could feel her heart pounding inside her chest, and knew I had to calm her down—and quickly. "How about we drive through Starbucks and get that pink drink you love so much?"

"I think that sounds amazing." She let my hand go so she could find some tissues to dry her tears and blow her nose. "I don't know how you can put up with my emotional meltdowns."

"You're not so bad." I had to laugh. "Some of the guys I know have horror stories about how their wives or girlfriends were when they were pregnant. You're like a walk in the park compared to those stories. I'm thankful for you."

Looking at me from the corner of her eyes, I saw a smile slowly take over her frown. "I'm extremely thankful for you."

"Yeah, I'm kind of a great guy," I joked.

"You *are* a totally great guy. Don't let anyone ever tell you otherwise." With a heavy sigh, she seemed to have calmed down and let everything else go. "So, a pink drink, and how about one of those little cake pops?"

"I think you deserve that and more. I'll have dinner delivered tonight from anywhere you want. You can have anything. Anything at all. Lobster. Duck. I don't want you to even look at the price of anything. You want it, you get it." I wanted to make her happy. I loved to see her smiling with that special light in her eyes.

Moving her hands over her stomach, she asked the baby, "Baby Patton, what would you like to eat for dinner?"

Baby Patton? Um, no. "Let's call him Patty. I always wanted to be called that, but no one ever would. My mother wouldn't let anyone call any of us by a nickname. I want our son to have a cute nickname."

"Patty it is then." She looked down at her tummy. "Do you like that?" Her eyes went wide as she reached for my hand. "He kicked!"

I rested my hand on her stomach then felt another kick. "Oh, my God! That's insane!" I knew right then and there that I wanted to be touching her tummy as much as I could.

After what the doctor said, it didn't sound like such a weird request. It sounded like I'd be doing pretty much everything for her from now on. So, a quick decision came to mind. "Things are going to change some at home."

"Like how?" She had her phone out, looking up the restaurants she could pick from. "Do you think French food is good?"

"I don't care for it. But if you'd like to give it a try, then we will." I wouldn't stop her from ever doing a thing she wanted.

"I don't know. It looks iffy. So, what things are going to change at home?" She swiped to go to the next screen, still searching.

"I'm going to sleep with you from here on out. In the same bed."

The way her jaw dropped told me I'd shocked her. "You're what?"

Well, looks like she's not into that idea at all.

20

ALEXA

AFTER THE SCORCHING SEX DREAM I'D HAD THE OTHER NIGHT, THE idea of Patton sleeping with me made me very nervous. But the pained expression on his handsome face made me even more uncomfortable. "I'll sleep on top of the blanket, Alexa. I didn't mean to make you think otherwise."

"It's just that I move a lot in my sleep," I came up with. Nodding, I went on, "I might kick you—you know, in the," I ran my hand in a circular motion to gesture to my private area, "family jewels."

Smiling, he lost the expression that bothered me so much. "Oh. Well, I'll just have to take my chances, I guess. It worried me when I woke up and heard you making those sounds, like you were in pain. I want to be right next to you, just in case you have another nightmare. That way I can wake you up before your body gets too stressed."

Holy moly! "How sweet of you." I didn't know what else to say to that. I hadn't been experiencing any pain in that dream, but maybe he was right. He could wake me up as soon as I started moaning and thrashing around. But then again, when he woke me up from a dream like that, I might just grab him and kiss him and do only the lord in Heaven knew what.

Pulling up to the gated entrance to what I now considered to be *our* home, he pushed the button on his visor to open it. "We've come this far; I don't want anything to happen to the baby." A grin pulled his lips up at the corners. "Patty. I don't want anything to happen to *Patty*."

"You have no idea how wonderful you are, do you?" I adored the man. My only wish was that I could let him know just how completely I did.

Parking the truck, he looked at me with what I could only describe as joy. "Do you know how wonderful you are?"

My cheeks heated as embarrassment swept through me. "Why, because I want to name our baby after you?"

"For that, and much, much more." His eyes darted to my hand, which had moved to the door handle. "You wait right there. You're not to walk further than to the bathroom and back, remember?"

As he got out of the truck, I had to wonder if he'd had a wheelchair delivered while we were away—he always seemed to be so prepared. Anticipating my every need. But he couldn't have, as the doctor had given us the orders as we were on our way home.

He opened the door then unbuckled my seatbelt. "I'll carry you inside."

"Patton, no." That was really too much. "I just walked into and out of the doctor's office. I can walk into the house."

"Nope." He scooped me up and carried me inside. "We *will* follow the doctor's orders to the letter."

It was hard for me to believe that anyone could be as perfect as Patton. "I suppose it will do no good to argue with you about this, so I'll just say thank you."

"You are very welcome." He took me inside then marched

me all the way to my bedroom. "I'll let you relax on your bed while I get things fixed up in my room for you. And I'll find a shower chair thingy and have it delivered too."

Apprehension filled me. "Your room?"

"Yes, I'm going to move you into my bedroom. I've got the bigger shower in there, with the jets that shoot out from everywhere. Plus, my bed is bigger, so that'll give you room to move around. I don't want you to be uncomfortable for even a moment." He put me on my bed then turned to leave. "I'm also going to order you some comfy clothes and pajamas. Your days of sleeping naked are over—for now." He turned and grinned at me, and it came off much sexier than I bet he realized. "And so are mine."

"I see." Taking a deep breath, I tried not to think about the night that lay ahead of us. I tried not to think about how much I appreciated and loved Patton. I tried not to think about how I would be able to hide my sexual attraction to him while we slept in the same bed. But it was impossible not to think about those things.

"You should take a nap while I get things ready for you." He closed the door, leaving me alone to wrestle with my inner thoughts.

I must've fallen asleep, because the next thing I knew I was waking up when I heard the door opening. He peeked inside. "You awake?"

Yawning, I stretched. "Yes. I guess I was more tired than I realized. I drifted off almost right away."

"I didn't want to say anything, but I could tell that you were tired. You haven't been getting much sleep, what with the nightmares and all." He walked in and went toward the bathroom. "I'm going to gather your toiletries and put them in the other bathroom. Then I'll come back to get you. Do you wanna hang out in the living room for a while?"

Being stuck in a bedroom for the next three months didn't sound appealing to me in the least. "Yes, I don't want to stay in one room too long. I think it'll depress me."

"I think you're right. We can sit outside some too. I've got those zero gravity chairs on the back deck." He stopped and held up one finger. "Oh. And pick out the place you want me to order dinner from."

I'd been dreaming about eating pizza. "I know you said that I can order from anywhere at all and not to worry about the price."

"And I mean that." He went into the bathroom then came out with an armload of toiletries. "I'll be right back."

"I want pizza," I shouted out after him.

When he came back, he put his hands on his hips, his lips pulling up to one side. "Pizza? Really?"

"Not just any pizza, Patton. I want one with grilled honey-glazed chicken breast, fresh grilled pineapple, sprinkled with kale." My mouth watered just thinking about it. "Chef Zorga makes it for me at the resort. Do you think you could tell him to make the Alexa special for me? He'll know what I want."

"I had no idea you were having a food affair with Zorga." He came and scooped me up into his strong arms. "Are there any other work-husbands I should be made aware of, wife?"

"No." I liked the hint of jealousy I'd seen in his blue eyes. "Are there any work-wives you have that I should know about?"

"I'm much too busy to be juggling two wives." He kissed my cheek. "And why would I bother with any other woman when I have the most gorgeous and sweetest wife at home?"

"Yes, why would you?" I asked with a smile.

Except for the lack of sex, our marriage felt very real. And now that we'd be sharing a bed, I felt that it would begin to get even more real. I was thrilled about that.

After dinner and watching a movie on television, the time

had come to go to bed. Butterflies swarmed my tummy as he climbed onto the bed, lying on top of the blanket. He grabbed the throw at the end of the bed to cover up with. "Night, Alexa. You make sure to wake me if you want anything."

Turning to lay on my side, I faced him. "I want you to sleep under the blanket with me. I don't want you to be uncomfortable either."

For a moment, he just looked into my eyes. "Alexa, I'll be fine. I don't want you to think you have to do anything to accommodate me."

"You are doing *everything* to accommodate me." I didn't like it being so one-sided. "I want you to be as comfortable as I am. And I want you to be able to feel this baby whenever you want to." I took his hand, placing it on the spot I'd just felt the baby kick. "Here, see if he'll kick for you. Talk to him." I loved when he spoke to the baby through my stomach.

Leaning over, he pressed his lips to my swollen tummy. Only a cotton nightgown separated his lips from my flesh. Flesh that burned with desire for him. "Daddy loves you. Can you hear me in there, Patty?"

The baby kicked, making us both smile. "See, I told you. He likes it when you talk to him. And he likes it when you put your hand on my stomach." And I liked it too. "Come on, get under the blanket with me." I turned to my other side as he got underneath the covers. "Here, lay behind me and rest your hand on my stomach."

Moving in behind me, his warm breath stirred my hair as he put his hands on me. "This isn't too intimate for you?" he asked with concern. "I don't want you to feel uncomfortable in any way."

The truth was that I loved feeling his body wrapped around mine. "You make me feel safe." *And loved.*

"You *are* safe with me." A long sigh came out of his mouth. "I like this."

"Me too." My eyes closed as a sense of calm spread over me. *I could do this every night—forever.* "I've never felt so comfortable in my life."

He snuggled up to me even closer. I could feel every part of his body against mine. It felt right. I felt whole in a way I never had before.

He is the right man for me. I just wish he and my brother could see that.

"Patton, I want you to know that I think you're the best man in this whole world. You've done so much for the baby and me. No one would do what you're doing. Not to the extent that you are. I just want you to know that I deeply appreciate you, and I will never stop. You aren't just my angel and my hero; you are my rock." I placed my hand over his as the baby kicked the spot just underneath his palm. "That's Patty's way of saying he feels the same way."

Warm lips pressed against my neck and I melted inside. "Not only is it my pleasure to be doing this, but I feel that you've given me a gift no one else could. Not only the gift of this child, but the gift of knowing and understanding you in ways I've never done with anyone else. The gift of your trust. I wouldn't change a thing about what we've done together."

A knot formed in my throat. I found such beauty in this simple act of sharing words of affection and care with each other while being so close, physically. If Patton hadn't had a dime, and we were lying on a mattress on the floor in some shack, I would still want to be with him, doing the same thing.

I'd never known much about love, but I knew this was it. There was no doubt in my mind. The only doubts I had were about my brother, and whether he would accept that this was what I wanted.

The way Patton held me, spoke to me, and the vibrations coming off him told me that he loved me the same way I loved him. It seemed that our mutual respect for my brother was all that was stopping us from taking that last step and confessing our feelings. But one day, one of us would have to find a way to let my brother know that we wanted to stay together and be a real husband and wife.

At least, I prayed that was how things would eventually work out. And after that, Patton and I could really begin. But for now, I had to accept that this was enough.

And this is pure bliss.

21

PATTON

"The doctor is coming over tomorrow," I told my younger brother, Warner, over the phone. "Alexa is thirty-six weeks now. Only four more to go."

"Seems like the end is near. How long are you guys planning on keeping up this marriage charade after the baby comes?" he asked me, making a knot form in my stomach with the thought of ending things with Alexa.

"We're not talking about anything like that right now. She can't have any stress. And I'm not worried about that anyway." I didn't want to get into things with him. I hadn't told anyone about my true feelings for Alexa—not even the woman herself. But I had told them how I felt about the baby. "It's not like I'm going to be in some kind of hurry to move my son out of my home."

"But he's not really *your* son," Warner reminded me.

Gritting my teeth, I hated the way everyone thought they had to point that out to me all the damn time. "I'll be the only father he will ever know, so he *is* my son." I had a feeling that my brothers were going to need a lecture on this subject.

"Whatever you say, bro." he chuckled as if it was a joke. "Anyway, I've got a courier going to your place. He's bringing over some papers you need to sign. If you can just sign them then send them back with him, I would be very thankful. Managing both the resort and spa side of this business is quite the handful."

I'd started doing a lot of work from home. But Warner, being the middle brother of the five of us, liked to act like he was being put out every time he possibly could. "And I thank you for your help. I'll be there for you when you need to take time off, too. I promise you."

"Just remember to take care of yourself too, Patton. You're bending over backwards for her and that baby. You've got to put yourself first some of the time."

"Not right now, I don't." He could never understand. He'd never been in love before. Not real love. Not the kind of love where you put the other person before everything else. "And I don't feel as if I'm bending at all. I feel like I'm doing exactly what I want to be doing."

"So, you *want* to be waiting on her hand and foot?" He chuckled as if I couldn't possibly want that.

"I don't consider it waiting on her hand and foot. I want to help her. I actually love doing it." I'd had no idea I would ever love taking almost complete care of someone, but I did. "Probably because she never *expects* me to do a thing for her, and she's always happy and grateful for everything I do. It helps when someone says thank you."

"Yeah, yeah," he said, sounding like he didn't believe a word I was saying. "Joe just texted me that he's at your gate. Go deal with that and I'll talk to you later."

"Okay." I was glad to get off the phone anyway.

It bothered me to no end that my brothers didn't understand what I was doing where Alexa and the baby were concerned. Perhaps if I'd been honest about being in love with her, it would make more sense to them. But when one has four brothers who haven't always known how to keep their mouths shut, and when one has a friend who can't find out the truth, one doesn't tell the brothers the biggest secret he's ever had.

The doorbell rang as I was on my way to it. Alexa lay on the sofa, her Kindle resting on her belly as she entertained herself by reading an e-book. She looked up at me as I headed to the door. "Are you expecting anyone?"

"Yeah. Warner sent over some papers for me to sign. Don't sit up. I won't bring Joe inside, so you can stay put." I knew she would try to make herself more presentable, instead of sprawling out on the sofa if she knew someone was going to see her that way. She often referred to herself as looking like a beached whale. If she was a beached whale, she was the cutest one I'd ever seen.

Out of the corner of my eye, I caught her smiling. "You're the best, Patton."

"I try to be." Opening the door, I stepped outside to deal with what Warner had sent over.

It only took me a few minutes to read the papers and sign them, and then I went back into the house only to find Alexa was not on the sofa anymore. Not thinking much about it, I went to the kitchen to see how dinner was coming along.

Following the doctor's orders, Alexa only got up to go to the bathroom, so I knew that was where she was. And I needed to get dinner finished. I'd made roasted chicken with pears and pearl onions. The internet had become my best source for recipes, and surprising Alexa with new dishes was one of my favorite things to do.

I knew my life had to sound boring to the average man; it was anything but that to me. And Alexa seemed happy, too. She never complained or even looked irritated about having to lie around all the time. But I knew it must've been taking a toll on her.

"Patton?" I heard her call out to me.

Turning off the oven, I went to see what she wanted. "Yes?"

"I just wanted to let you know I'm going to take a shower." She stood in the doorway of the kitchen, her hand on her back. "My back's killing me from lying around so much. So I'm just going to let the hot water work its magic on my sore muscles. How long until dinner's ready?"

"It'll be ready for you whenever you get out of the shower. No need to rush. I'll lay out something comfortable for you to sleep in, and I'll bring dinner to bed." I moved along with her, seeing her to the bedroom. "Other than the back pain, is everything else alright?"

"I guess so." She rubbed her back, wincing with pain. "I'm just feeling worn out. Who would've thought that lying around for a couple of months could wear me out?"

I knew it was hard on her. She tried to make it seem as if it didn't bother her at all. But I knew it did. "It's not easy to be so completely immobile." I hated seeing pain on her face. "Just get into the shower and let those jets get to work." I kissed the top of her head. "I'm glad I found that shower chair with the back on it, so you're more comfortable in there."

"Me too." Even in pain, she managed a smile. "I'll feel better soon. Thank you, mi amor."

Stopping at the door, I leaned against the frame and watched her walk slowly away from me. My heart felt as if it melted inside my chest as emotions swirled inside of me. Love. Empathy. Sorrow.

It saddened me to think about Alexa losing her virginity to a man who didn't love her. It was sad that she'd become pregnant by a man who didn't love her. And it was sad that she wasn't having a good pregnancy.

One good thing was that we'd finished the nursery and ordered everything we needed for the baby's arrival online. It had all come in already, and I'd put everything where it needed to be. We were ready for Patty's arrival, although no one wanted him to come too early.

Patiently, we waited, letting him grow where he'd grow best. But it was sad to see the pain Alexa was in. She was already having such a hard start to motherhood. Yet, she still had no complaints and looked forward to being a mom.

Going back to the kitchen, I got the rest of dinner ready then plated up our food. Putting it on a tray, I covered the plates with silver domes to keep the food warm. I'd bought a portable tray for Alexa, like the ones they have in hospitals. It made it easier for her to eat while keeping her feet up. I'd done everything I could to make things as pleasant for her as they could be.

I'd changed into my pajamas and gotten into bed already, waiting to eat dinner with her. When she emerged from the bathroom, she didn't look a whole lot better than when she'd gone in. "I've got dinner ready for you. Come get into bed and I'll take care of everything else."

"It smells amazing." She winced as she got into bed. "The shower helped some, but not much. I just want to eat then snuggle down in this bed with you at my back. The pressure your body puts on my back always makes it feel better."

"Glad to be of service, my lady." I loved sleeping with her. What was odd to me was that holding her all night long without getting aroused hadn't been hard to do at all. I supposed it was because I knew she couldn't have sex anyway, so there wasn't any reason to work myself up over something that just couldn't happen.

She wasted no time, eating the food then snuggling down, turning to lie on her side. "Thank you for dinner. As always, it was exceptional. Once I've got this baby on the outside of my body, I swear to you that I'll return all of this kindness you've shown me. I'll take over all the cooking and get to pamper you for once."

"Sounds great to me. But you know what I think will work even better for us?" I didn't want to put the chores all on her shoulders. "I think we should alternate. I'll cook a couple of days of the week and you can too, and then we'll order out a few days. That way we both get free nights."

"Sounds good to me." She grabbed my hand as soon as I got into bed. "Now wrap yourself around me and make this backache go away."

"My pleasure." Moving in close, I rested my hand on her stomach and in no time at all, we both fell asleep.

Sometime later, I woke to a soft moan. Coming to my sense, I felt something very strange going on underneath my hand, as her stomach felt hard as a rock. Alexa's entire body went stiff as a board for about twenty seconds then it went soft again, as did her stomach. Her moaning stopped and was replaced by soft snores.

I'd been reading up on labor and felt sure that had been a contraction. But I didn't want to wake her unless another one happened. Lying still, I waited for quite some time before the same thing happened.

It lasted twenty seconds again. So, I turned over and picked up my phone off the nightstand so I could see how far apart these things were coming—if she had another one.

Twenty minutes later, there came another one, and this time I knew I had to make the call to the doctor. Getting out of bed as quietly as I could, I left the bedroom to make the call.

"Patton?" the doctor answered, sounding sleepy.

"I know it's the middle of the night, doc, but I'm fairly sure that Alexa's having contractions in her sleep. Her stomach gets hard, her entire body tenses up, and she moans." Closing my eyes, I tried to calm myself down as panic began rising up inside of me. "I know this is too early for the baby to come."

"Do you know how long the contractions are and how much time is between them?"

"They are twenty minutes apart, and they last twenty seconds. She's only had three that I'm aware of. There may have been more before I woke up though." I knew this wasn't good. "He'll be like four weeks early if he's born now."

"Look, I don't want you to worry. Keep her calm. That's your job, Daddy. Keep her calm and wake her up gently then grab your hospital bag and take her to Saint David's. I'll let them know you're coming. You'll have to go in through the emergency room entrance. I'll be there soon." She paused. "You've got this, Patton. No worries."

Holy shit, it's happening. Being a father looks like it might be a lot harder than I thought it would be!

22

ALEXA

Holding my stomach with both hands as another contraction wracked my body, I wished we were already at the hospital, instead of on the way there. "How did I sleep through something this painful?"

"I don't know, but you did." Patton put on his hazard lights. "I'm going to speed up. I don't like seeing you in pain at all."

Breathing again as the contraction eased off, I took out my phone and called my brother. "Alexa?"

"Luciano, we're on the way to the hospital. I think the baby's coming." I closed my eyes as I thought about the fact that my mother couldn't be there with me for the birth of her first grandchild. "It'll be best for Mamma not to know until after I have the baby. I don't want her to be stressed out."

"I agree," he said. "And I'm going to get dressed and meet you at the hospital. I'll text Patton when I get there so he can direct me to you. I will see you soon, my princesa."

"I love you, hermano." As I put my cell into my purse, I sniffled as a few tears slipped from my eyes. "It's upsetting that my mother can't be with me."

"I know it is." He ran his hand over my shoulder. "But we

both know how stressed out she'd be. And then there's the fact that she might accidentally hear that the baby's actually only a month early, instead of the two months she'll think he is."

"Yes, I know. I can't let our secret get out now. And I would never want her to be worried. After he's born, I'll call her with the good news. I hope it'll all be good news." Worry filled me about him being four weeks early.

Rubbing my shoulder, Patton tried to help. "The doc said things have been looking good for our boy. I'm sure he'll be fine. Maybe a little on the small side, but fine."

Nodding, I hoped he was right. "I just want things to go well."

"Me too." Patton pulled into the parking lot by the emergency entrance. Only a couple of cars were parked there. "I'll go get a wheelchair. You wait right here."

Sitting in the truck as he went inside, I looked up, clasped my hands, and offered a prayer to the Virgin Mary, asking for her help through the birth of my child.

After the prayer, I thought about how she'd sort of been in my situation. Her baby was not Joseph's son. And she hadn't been married to Joseph when she'd conceived her baby. Joseph had married her to make sure she was cared for, and her baby would be too. And their marriage would keep her reputation in check.

Joseph knew Jesus wasn't his child, and he still loved him and raised him as his own son. Of course, Jesus' father wasn't able to be on Earth, raising him. But the situation was very much the same.

Patton was every bit as selfless as Joseph was. I smiled as he came back to me, rolling the wheelchair in front of him. Both were loving men who were good to their families. I knew Patton would be good to my son. I knew it without a doubt. He was every bit the father that Joseph was.

As he opened the door, I had to let him know how highly I thought of him. "Patton, before we get inside and around others, I just want you to know that I think you're the best man in the world and this baby and I are extremely lucky to have you."

Running his fingertips along my cheek, tears shimmered in his eyes. "Funny, I was just going to tell you that I think you're the best woman in the world and that this baby and I are the luckiest couple of guys in the world to have you. Seems great minds think alike." He smiled at me. "Now climb aboard, my lady. Your chariot awaits."

Wiping my eyes, I tried to push my emotions to the side as he helped me get onto the wheelchair. "So, this is it. The doctor didn't say she was going to give me anything to try to stop the contractions, right?"

"She didn't say anything to me about doing that," he said as he pushed me toward the sliding glass doors of the ER. "But that doesn't mean she won't. We'll just have to see what she thinks needs to be done. Either way, I think we'll be here for a while. I don't think we'll be going home until we've got a baby to take with us."

The doors swooshed open at three in the morning on a Saturday in May. An empty lobby greeted us as he wheeled me down a long hallway into the hospital's main lobby.

We'd come to check out the hospital a month ago, so Patton knew exactly where he was going. Onto the elevator we went, up to the third floor. Getting off the elevator, we were only a short walk away from the nurses' station in the labor and delivery department.

A nurse stepped into the hallway from one of the patient's rooms. "Are you the Nash's?"

"We are," Patton said.

She waved us over. "Come over here. This will be your birthing room. I just finished getting it ready for you." She went over to the bed to pick up a pale blue hospital gown. "Okay, Daddy, I'll let you get this on Mommy and then you can get her into bed. Do me a favor and press the nurses' button on the side rail and I'll come in to hook her up to everything."

"Do you know if the doctor is going to try to stop the contractions?" I wanted to know if I would be having the baby soon or not.

"She hasn't ordered Terbutaline, so I don't think she wants to stop it. You're at thirty-six weeks, so that's not much of a problem." The nurse eyed my stomach. "My bets are on that baby boy weighing close to six pounds, if not a hair over that."

"Really?" That made me feel a lot better. I'd read that babies had to weigh over four pounds to be able to leave the hospital. And it sounded like mine was a good amount over that weight.

"Yep," the nurse said. "In general, most babies at thirty-six weeks tend to be around five pounds."

I'd had two contractions on the drive over and now another one was ramping up. I put my hands on either side of my stomach. "Here comes another one."

Patton pulled out his cell to check the time. "Still twenty minutes apart. Let's see how long it lasts."

I counted silently as I took long, slow, deep breaths through the whole thing. "Twenty seconds."

The nurse nodded. "Good. You two make quite the team."

"Yes, we do," I had to agree.

She left us alone and Patton went to get the gown off the bed then came back to me. "Ready or not, here we go."

"You know, I think this will be okay after all." I began to feel a lot better about the whole thing. "I think we're going to be fine." I meant all of us—as a family. "I've just got this very positive feeling right now."

"Everything *will* be fine." He looked at the buttons of my pajama top. "Get rid of the top first. I'll get this on you, then you can drop the bottoms and your panties. I'll help you get into the bed after that."

For some strange reason, I didn't feel the least bit uncomfortable or shy about having him help me with this. Maybe sleeping together had helped rid me of my insecurities. Whatever it was, I was extremely grateful that I felt calm and relaxed with him.

In no time at all, I was in bed with an IV attached to my arm, a monitor wrapped around my belly, and a host of other lines attached to my chest and tummy. I looked at my hospital ID bracelet. *Mrs. Alejandra Nash.*

The nurse had put one on Patton too. He had to have one in order to show that he was the father of the baby. He looked at it with such an odd stare. I saw fear, wonder, and above all, I saw pride.

He had every right to have pride in himself for what he'd done so far. "You know that you're going to be the best father ever, right?"

Looking at me, he just smiled. "I'll have to be if I'm going to come close to comparing to how amazing a mother you'll be."

The door opened and in walked my brother. "I made it."

"In record time," Patton said as he went to hug him. "I'm glad you're here, brother."

"I'm glad you are too," Luciano said as he winked at me over Patton's shoulder. They ended the hug, my brother's eyes on me. "Patton, do you think you could find me some coffee? I don't know my way around this place. I don't think I'd be able to find some and be back in time to see my nephew born."

"Yeah, I'll grab you a cup." He left the room, leaving my brother and me alone.

I had the idea he'd sent Patton on the errand just so he could talk to me in private. As he came and sat on the side of my bed, I knew he wanted to talk about something important. "How are things?"

"Good." I didn't know what he was going to say, but I hoped he wouldn't tell me some nonsense about ending the fake marriage soon. I didn't want to think about that at all right now.

"I wanted to say that I've been wrong." He closed his eyes as he took my hand. "See, I've wanted to see things in a different way than they really are. And I've finally realized that what I've wanted is wrong."

I still had no idea what he was getting at. "What have you been wrong about?" I hoped he didn't mean asking Patton to marry me. Because that had been the rightest thing ever.

"He loves you. I can see that now. And as I've told you before, I've already seen that you love him. So, I am saying that I've been wrong about you two. And whatever you two decide to do, I approve of." He leaned over, kissed my forehead then sighed. "You're a grown woman who is smart and able to decide who you want to be with. So, I am leaving it up to you, mi princesa."

He thinks Patton loves me!

"Thank you." I tried not to cry but failed. I hadn't realized that Patton looked at me the way my brother saw. I had been hopeful, I had thought I'd felt our connection growing, but I still had the idea that I was the only one in love. Hearing that my brother saw the same thing in his very best friend in the whole world made me feel ecstatic.

I wasn't about to try to have the conversation with Patton right here and right then, but at least I knew that when we did have time to discuss the future of us, we had my brother's blessing.

Though I was overjoyed at the thought of having that conversation, I knew I had other things to focus on at the moment—like giving birth to a healthy baby.

23

PATTON

Seventeen hours—that's how long Alexa was in labor. Grueling, and at times torturous, the pain seemed to take her over completely at the end. But still, she refused any type of pain medication.

She is the strongest woman I've ever known.

For the last few hours, she'd been sleeping peacefully. She'd finally allowed them to give her something for the pain, once the baby was outside of her body. She wasn't about to let anything harm the baby in any way. But once she didn't have the baby to worry about anymore, she wanted something—anything—to get rid of the pain. The Vicodin took her under almost immediately. I was immensely glad for it as I watched them stitch her up and hook her up to a bag of Pitocin to keep her uterus contracting to help stop the bleeding.

She'd lost a lot of blood, so they wanted to stop the bleeding as soon as they possibly could. The doctor even said they might have to give her a pint or two of blood to help make up for the loss.

Alexa was pale, her lips were colorless. I'd never seen her look so weak. But I knew she would recover from this with some tender loving care. And I intended to care for her the way I had since the beginning. I would make sure she got back to a hundred percent—sooner, rather than later.

The baby began moving around as he lay in the little, clear bassinet at the foot of the bed. Getting up, I went to see to him. He weighed five pounds and ten ounces. Still a tiny baby, but not as tiny as some premature babies. Plus, he'd shown good lung function, the thing that had concerned the pediatrician the most. Patty had come out screaming at the top of his little lungs, which they said was a good thing. It meant he was breathing on his own.

Making little grunts, he moved his head back and forth. The nurse had left a pacifier for him, should he want to suckle while Alexa was still sleeping. Gently, I picked him up, cradling him in one arm as I picked up the pacifier and put it to his lips. He pulled it into his mouth right away. I thought that was a sign he'd take to breastfeeding no problem.

Alexa had already set her mind on breastfeeding. I hoped Patty would go along with her on that and not make things too tough on her. She'd had it rough for such a long time already. It was time things began to ease up for her.

With the birth of the baby and everything I'd watched Alexa go through, I knew I couldn't hold off on talking to Luci about my feelings for his sister any longer. I hadn't thought I could love her more, but watching her give birth—to *our* baby—had set my heart on fire.

My plan was to get Luci's blessing then let Alexa know how I felt. And I had high hopes that she would let me know that she felt the same way. We could focus on being a real couple—a real family. There'd be no more talk of a divorce.

Sitting down in the rocking chair next to the bed, I couldn't pull my eyes off the little bundle in my arms. He had on a beanie with blue and white stripes and was wrapped in a baby blue blanket. Even with puffy eyes and a wrinkled forehead, he was the most precious thing I'd ever seen in my life. "You know what, Patty? Daddy loves you very, very much, and always will."

It was impossible not to fall in love with him. Just as impossible as it had been not to fall in love with his mother. Those two had done me in. They'd captured my heart in ways I hadn't known possible. And I loved every bit about it.

Looking at his little hospital bracelet, I saw my name there. *Father—Patton Nash.*

My heart felt heavier than it ever had—but in the best way. It was so full that it would just have to get used to the added weight of love this little boy filled it with. Looking at Alexa, I smiled. "You did good, babe. You did real good."

She was still out like a light and didn't even stir at the sound of my voice. I watched her for a moment, her chest rising and falling slowly. Labor and delivery had worn her out completely.

I had no idea how women did it. It made no sense at all to think that men were the stronger sex. There was no way I could see me or any other man going through the absolute hell Alexa had. I honestly thought I would die during that process had our roles been reversed. It seemed to be more than what a human body could endure.

Being with Alexa had changed me for the better. She hadn't meant to or even tried to, but her presence rubbed off on me, made me nicer, more caring—and not nearly as cynical as I had been.

Gazing at the first and only newborn I'd ever held in my life, I knew our son would make an even bigger difference in the man I'd been. Not that I had ever thought about it before, but I wanted to teach our son how to throw and catch a ball. I wanted to teach him how to ride a bike. I wanted to teach him how to swim, play golf, and climb trees. I wanted to be with him for as many firsts as I could. Not a minute would be wasted with him.

Looking at the still sleeping Alexa, I thought something seemed off about her. I watched her for a moment then it hit me. *Her breathing has slowed.*

The quiet, steady beat of the heart monitor suddenly turned into one long sound. I stood with the baby still in my arms. "Alexa? Honey?"

A stampede of people clad in different colored scrubs careened into the room. "Code blue. Repeat, code blue maternity two, zero, two," blasted over the intercom.

Her heart's not beating. "Alexa! Alexa, wake up!" I held the baby close to me as more and more people came into the room, converging on his mother.

One of the female nurses climbed onto the bed, straddling her, and then put her fists together before pounding them on Alexa's unmoving chest. "Come on, girl!" she shouted. "You've got lots to live for!"

"AED, one minute out," one of the male nurses shouted.

I wasn't sure what that meant, but guessed it meant the machine they use to fix a troubled heart. "Alexa! Come on, baby! Stay with me! Stay with us!"

More pounding on her chest followed, as the nurses took turns trying to get Alexa's heart back to normal. Then a large male nurse who was built like a linebacker took his turn. His deep voice rattled the room as he pulled his mighty fists up high. "You're going to make it, ma'am."

BAM! Her eyes flew open as the heart monitor made a beat and then another.

"Alexa!" I shouted. "Stay with us!"

Her eyes searched the crowded room until she found me. "Patton," she smiled softly. "You'll take care of our son," her voice sounded weak. And then her eyes closed, and the beating of her heart stopped again.

"No!" I couldn't believe it. "Alexa, come back! Don't go! I can't do this without you!"

Someone took me by the shoulders, gently urging me to walk into the hallway as two more nurses pushed the machine in that I prayed would get her heart back to normal for good. "Stay out here, sir. We'll do all we can for her. But you need to take care of that baby."

I moved backward until my back hit the wall, dazed and in shock. "I can't lose her." I looked at the baby who somehow slept soundly in my arms. "Patty, we can't lose her. I can't do this by myself. I just can't."

I heard the sound of the elevator doors opening from down the hall and looked over. Luciano stepped off, blue balloons in one hand, a vase of red roses in the other. His eyes went wide as he saw me standing there, holding the baby. "Patton? What the hell is going on?"

"She's..." I didn't want to say it out loud and could only shake my head.

He ran to me, tossing the flowers onto the nearby desk of the nurses' station while letting the balloons go. "She's what?" He darted past me, trying to get into the room, but it was packed with people. "She's my sister. What's happening?" The loud zap of the electric paddles on her chest sent him stumbling backward. "No," he whispered. "No, this can't be."

"Her heart stopped," I finally managed to say. "I don't know what happened. She was breathing fine and then she wasn't breathing at all. I was sitting there next to her with the baby in my arms when she flatlined." I had to stop talking, a knot forming in my throat.

"How could this happen?" Luci asked as he looked up. "You can't let this happen to her."

I couldn't let one more second go by without telling the truth. "Luci, I'm sorry. I really am. I never meant to betray your trust. And I haven't done a thing about my feelings for her. But —God help me, I love your sister. I want our marriage to be real. I don't want to ever lose her. I hope you can learn to forgive me. I'm not going to let another day go by without telling her my true feelings. She has to come out of this. She just has to."

His eyes went soft as he nodded. "You have my blessing, brother." He held out his hand. "Let us join hands and pray."

Holding Patty in one arm, I held Luciano's hand with the other. "Virgin Mary, please hear our prayers," I began as I knew no other who would be as quick to help Alexa than the mother of our savior.

My best friend and I prayed hard and faithfully as he added, "Alejandra Consuelo Christina De La Cruz-Nash is needed here on Earth. Her son and husband need her with them to grow as a family."

My heart pounded so hard inside my chest, I feared it might burst right out of it. "Please don't take her away from us. I will cherish her always." It hit me that Alexa's parents and brother had always thought of her as their angel, since she'd had her troubles coming into the world. "She is our angel right here on Earth. Please allow us to keep her for a while longer."

My legs felt as if they might give out and leave me on the floor in a puddle of despair. But faith, hope, and the knowledge that many people were in there right now trying their best to keep her with us made me stand tall, certain that she would come through this.

I refused to listen to what was going on inside the room. I only listened to the sounds of Luciano's voice and mine as we each prayed at the same time for her to stay with us.

We were not about to let her go. We were not about to call it quits and give into death. She was too young, too strong, and too loved.

I had no idea what had happened to her, but I knew the

medical staff had seen this sort of thing before and knew what needed to be done to bring her back. None of them were ready to see her go either.

I began swaying back and forth, rocking the baby as I whispered, praying constantly, "We will not let her go. Please, help her. Please, help *us*."

Her brother and I held hands tightly, neither of us willing to stop praying until she was out of danger. She had a place in our hearts and held ours in hers as well. We were bonded, connected, and nothing—not even death—could break those bonds.

I held our son, knowing that he had to have the chance to know his mother. She was the most wonderful person on the planet. He had to meet her—get to know her—fall in love with her. He was meant for this world. He was meant to bring Alexa and I together. Patty was our fate. And fate couldn't end before it even got a chance to begin.

Whatever I had to do, I wouldn't let Alexa go. If prayers didn't work, I'd do everything else in my power to help her come out of this. No one would ever stop me from trying.

You can't go, my love. You can't leave me now. I won't let you go.

24

ALEXA

I felt as if chaos surrounded me, so I moved to get away from it–moved upward. My body felt so light, too light, like a balloon filled with helium. Drifting toward the ceiling, the light above me began to glow brighter and brighter until I couldn't see a thing.

"It's not working," I heard a woman say from somewhere below me.

I didn't want to listen to all those noisy people. I didn't want to hear what they had to say. I just wanted them to be quiet and calm down.

"She's my sister. What's happening?" I heard my brother shout, his voice sounded shaky. I'd never heard such fear in his voice before.

A loud zapping sound jolted me for a moment, stopping me from rising any higher. Turning over, I faced the floor and saw all the people huddled in the middle of the room.

The room I'd given birth in not long ago.

"No," I heard my brother whisper. "No, this can't be." Although I could hear him, I couldn't see him. I moved toward the sound, wanting to see Luciano.

"Her heart stopped," I heard Patton say.

Whose heart stopped?

I had no idea what he was talking about, but I had the idea that he was talking to my brother. So, I followed the sound of his voice as Patton went on. "I don't know what happened. She was breathing fine and then she wasn't breathing at all."

Who wasn't breathing?

Feeling confused, I suddenly felt desperate to see the faces of Patton and my brother.

Patton went on to say, "I was sitting there next to her with the baby in my arms when she flatlined."

The baby! Is he talking about Patty?

"How could this happen? You can't let this happen to her," I heard my brother cry out with so much agony in his voice that it hurt me to think of him being in that much pain.

"Luci, I'm sorry. I really am," Patton said. "I never meant to betray your trust. And I haven't done a thing about my feelings for her. But—God help me, I love your sister."

He loves me?

"I want our marriage to be real."

He wants a real marriage?

"I don't want to ever lose her."

Why does he think he'll ever lose me? I would never leave him.

"I hope you can learn to forgive me," he said to my brother. "I'm not going to let another day go by without telling her my true feelings. She has to come out of this. She just has to."

She? Is he talking about me?

I finally moved to the door then ducked and was able to go through it. And there I saw my brother and Patton. Patton held our son in his arms, a look of pure anguish on his handsome face.

Luciano looked at Patton with admiration. "You have my blessing, brother."

I'd already known that my brother had given me his blessing, and now Patton had it too. Nothing stood in our way of becoming a happy family now.

Luciano held out his hand to Patton. "Let us join hands and pray."

What is there to pray about? And for who? I couldn't recall ever feeling so completely confused in my life.

I watched as Patton took my brother's hand and held our son in the other arm. "Virgin Mary, please hear our prayers."

My brother added, "Alejandra Consuelo Christina De La Cruz-Nash is needed here on Earth."

Me? It's me they're praying for?

I felt dazed as I continued to watch them pray, no longer hearing their words, but sensing the desperation behind their pleas. I couldn't stand this anymore—they needed to know I would never leave them. "Hey, I'm here!" I shouted. But neither of them looked at me. I figured it was because I was floating above them. So, I reached out, trying to grab Patton, the taller of the two men, to use him to pull myself down to the floor so they could see me.

Waving my hand through the air, I managed to get to him and grabbed his shoulder. He shuddered and stepped away from me, looking at the empty space beside him with wide eyes.

"What's wrong?" Luciano asked him. "You look like you've seen a ghost."

"Something cold touched just my shoulder." Patton looked around, even straight up at me, but he didn't seem to be able to see me.

Am I dead?

That would certainly explain the floating. Closing my eyes, I tried not to cry. I had to stop this from happening. I couldn't be dead. I wouldn't be in this hallway if I were dead. I'd be on my way to Heaven.

Unless my sin has caused me to stay in limbo.

I hadn't made a confession about what I'd done with Alejandro. And now it was too late to do anything about it.

Or was it?

I watched as Patton's eyes moved around, as if he searched for something. "Alexa, I love you. I want us to be man and wife for real. I want us to raise our son together. I want us to be a real family and I never want to let you go. So, please, please, stay with us. Don't leave us. Not now. Not ever. And I swear to the lord above that I will never leave you."

"I love you, Patton," I shouted.

A sense of determination settled into every ounce of my being—or whatever being was left of me as I floated in this limbo. I wasn't dead yet, and I'd be damned if I'd let anything take me away from the man of my dreams and my son.

A sudden jolt of pure heat hit me square in the chest, and I felt as if I was being yanked back into the room. It felt as if I was body-slammed onto the bed, and then white-hot pain scorched my entire body. "Ahhh! It hurts! It hurts! Make it stop!"

"We've got her back," I heard a man say.

And then I saw Patton and Luciano run into the room as Patton shouted, "You stay with us, Alexa Nash! I love you!"

It all came rushing back to me. *He loves me!* "I'm not going anywhere. I love you too, Patton Nash." The pain in my chest was on the scope of unbearable. "You've got to stop this pain," I begged the doctor who stood over me.

He looked at me with concern and sympathy. "I know it hurts. But the pain will soon fade. It's from the electric shock we had to use to get your heart back on track."

Suddenly, the jolts I'd felt made sense. "Oh. Okay." How could I be upset when they'd done it to bring me back to life? "Do you know why my heart stopped in the first place?"

"Well, not yet," the doctor told me. "But we'll find that out."

As everyone began moving back and leaving the room, Patton came to me, our sleeping baby still in his arms. His warm lips pressed against my forehead, sending chills through me. "I've got my suspicions it was the pain medication. So, try not to take any more of that."

The doctor made a grim face. "Yes, we won't be using that on you anymore. We'll go ahead and place a warning about that on your chart, too. No more Vicodin for you, Mrs. Nash."

I didn't recognize the doctor at all. "I'm sorry, doctor. You are?"

"Doctor Levy. I'm on call here today. I'll be sure to make a full report for Doctor Barclay." He looked at the baby, who'd begun to squirm in Patton's arms while making a little fussing sound. "Are you breastfeeding?"

"I haven't had the opportunity yet, but that is my plan." I held out my hands for the baby. "Looks like he's getting hungry though."

"Yes, it does look that way," the doctor agreed. "But I don't think you should breastfeed him right now. Your heart did stop beating for almost three minutes. All you need to worry about right now is getting some rest and recovering your strength. I'm shocked you're even conscious right now."

"That makes sense," I said as my eyes started drooping. I wasn't too happy about it, but I had to do what was best for me or I wouldn't be able to do anything for anyone else. And I had lots to do.

"I'll send in a nurse with a bottle of formula," the doctor said then left.

Patton and Luciano stood there, staring at me. It all felt like a weird dream now. "So, that was something. Sorry I scared you guys," I murmured, fighting off sleep for a little while longer.

The nurse came in and handed Patton a small bottle. "Feed him a half ounce then stop and burp him. And make sure you pat his back until he burps before you give him another half ounce. It's important that you do that or he's going to get gas. Gas makes babies fussy, and fussy babies are no fun at all. If you need anything, just press the nurses' button on the side rail of the bed." She turned her attention to me. "How are you feeling?"

It was an odd feeling that was hard to describe. But then it hit me. "Like lightning struck me."

She nodded. "Yeah, I get that a lot when I ask someone who's just been shocked back to life. It wears off faster than you'd think. Let me know if you need anything."

As I looked into her green eyes a sudden burst of sadness overcame me and I began crying. "I died, didn't I?"

Moving quickly, she took my hand, gently rubbing the top of it. "Sort of, but not really. This is a traumatic event, and you should know that you will have some emotions about what's happened to you. Your doctor will do some tests to find out why your heart stopped. You may have an underlying condition that you and your doctor weren't aware of. But don't worry about that or anything else right now. You're okay and safe."

Wiping my eyes, I felt so strange. "I'll be okay." Looking at Patton and then my brother, I knew I had a couple of great men looking out for me. "I've got a great support team."

"You certainly do," she agreed. "So, let your hubby take care of the baby while you rest."

Another bout of strong sadness took me over and I started to cry again. "I wanted to breastfeed."

"And you will still get a chance to do that. For now, though, you've gotta take care of you and let Daddy feed and take care of the baby. I don't want you to worry about a thing." Looking at Patton, she nodded at the rocking chair. "Take a seat, Daddy. Rock that baby and keep things nice and calm for Mamma."

"Will do. I don't want anything taking her away from us." He smiled at me. "Because we all love you. Especially me."

Aww, he loves me. My heart skipped a beat and they all heard it, turning their heads to the heart monitor in panic. I knew it was nothing to be worried about, though—it was just the effect he had on me. "As you can hear, I love you too."

Lying in that bed, gazing at my husband as he fed our baby boy, I imagined that this must be what Heaven would feel like. But I was glad I was here on this Earth instead. Whatever the reason for my heart stopping, I knew if my doctor couldn't figure it out, then Patton would find a doctor who could.

I closed my eyes as sadness tried to take me under again. *I cannot cry again. I am alive, I am loved, and I have a healthy baby. I can't ask for more.*

25

PATTON

Three days later, and the doctors finally had enough test results to diagnose why Alexa's heart had stopped. As I'd predicted, the Vicodin was to blame. It turns out she'd had an allergic reaction.

We were happy with the findings because it meant that Alexa didn't have an underlying heart condition that we would have to worry about dealing with in years to come. With her mother's heart trouble, it had been weighing heavily on our minds that she too might have a similar problem.

Luciano would be bringing his parents up to stay a few days with us in the near future. They all wanted us to get home and settled before coming for a visit. Of course, no one had told them that Alexa's heart had stopped, for fear of her mother's reaction. They thought we'd had to stay at the hospital because of the baby's early arrival.

As we prepared to leave, I packed the bag we'd brought to the hospital with us when we'd come. But my brothers and people from work had come to visit and each one of them had brought presents for the baby and Alexa, so I had lots more to carry out than I'd had to carry in. "I'm going to have to make a few trips, babe."

"I've got our little pumpkin butt right here," she said as she pulled her shirt back into place after giving Patty a little dinner before we got on the road home.

We were both over the moon that he'd taken to the breast with no problems at all. He'd taken both the bottle and the breast, which the nurses told us wasn't always the case with most babies, especially newborns.

Just before I got to the door, a knock came and then a man I recognized stepped inside. "Mr. and Mrs. Nash, I'm Deacon Soliz." He looked back and forth at us, seeming to recognize us too. "Hold on a moment. Don't I know you?" He shook his finger at me. "You came to my home." He looked at Alexa. "To find you, Alexa. Oh, my goodness! How have you been?" He smiled at her. "I see you've been busy since you left us. Married and with a baby already." He smiled with what looked like genuine happiness for his former boarder.

Though he seemed to be grateful for this happy reunion, my mind snapped as I thought about the fact that Patty's grandfather was standing right there. His real, flesh and blood grandfather. Panic rushed through me. "I'll let you two catch up while I take these things to the car, babe." I couldn't be in the same room with the man. So many thoughts flooded my mind.

As I walked out of the room, I heard Alexa say, "We did have a baby. He's a little early, but he's healthy as they come. How have you and Mrs. Soliz been?"

Going to the elevator, I felt my pulse speeding up and my breathing becoming rapid. *Just calm down.*

I felt on the verge of a panic attack or something—it was something I'd never felt before. There was absolutely no reason for me to feel guilty about anything, but there I was feeling guilty anyway.

The coincidence of that man coming in to make a religious visit with the family of his biological grandson was just too much. What were the chances of that happening?

We'd been visited by a person from the clergy each day while in the hospital. And just as we were about to leave, here comes Patty's grandfather. It had to be fate stepping in.

I made it down to the main floor and out to the parking lot, where I loaded our stuff into the trunk of Alexa's car. She'd wanted me to bring it rather than my truck, as she said she didn't want to have to climb up into the passenger seat and maybe rip her stitches. Her car was okay, but I already had plans on buying her something much safer since she would be driving with a baby on board now.

As I closed the trunk and went back to get more, I couldn't stop myself from wondering what I would feel like if I had a grandson in the world that I knew nothing about.

But the situation with Alejandro was different. Alexa had told him about the baby and he'd told her to get rid of it. But his parents didn't know a damn thing about the pregnancy. I found it unfair that they weren't given a chance to say if they wanted to be in their grandson's life or not. Knowing their religious affiliation, I thought they would probably want to be in his life, regardless of what their son had said and done.

Alexa and I hadn't discussed anything about the Soliz family in a long time. Alexa had said before that they'd raised Alejandro, a womanizing liar who didn't care if she murdered his baby, so why would she want his parents in her son's life. So, I was quite sure her take on things would still be the same.

But maybe her mind had changed since having the baby. Maybe the man's visit would have her feeling the same guilt I did. So, I hurried back to the room, only to find him gone. "How'd that go?"

"Fine," she said as if it wasn't a big deal at all. "The nurse said they're about to bring in the release papers and after we sign them, we can go. I'm so ready to be home. Aren't you?"

I was more than ready to be out of that hospital. It was nice, but it wasn't home. "Of course I'm ready to be home." I couldn't believe how nonchalant she was being about the grandfather of her baby being in the same room with him. "Did you say anything to him about Patty?"

Her eyes shot daggers at me. "Are you being serious right now?"

Maybe not.

"You know what? I'll just grab this next bunch of things and take them to the car. I'll be right back to get the last load and hopefully they'll have the paperwork ready by then." I took off, not wanting to look her in the eyes after that response.

I'd never seen that look from her before. It was more than a little scary. But, like they say, a mother can become a bear in a heartbeat if she feels she needs to.

There was no way that I wanted to upset Alexa. But I also didn't think I could just keep my mouth shut about things either. Perhaps the deacon and his wife deserved to know about their grandson. Perhaps they would become an intricate part of his life. And maybe that would be for the best. After all, the more people who would love our child, the better. Or so I thought, anyway.

After putting away three loads in the trunk of the car, completely filling it up, I headed back up to Alexa to find her signing papers. "Oh, good, you're back." She slid the stack of papers over then handed me the pen. "I've just finished signing them. Now it's your turn."

"Why do they need all this signed by both of us?" I began putting my John Hancock on the papers. "I've already given them the insurance information and even paid the co-pay already. What is all this?"

"Odds and ends," she said as she put Patty into the car seat.

"The trunk is packed to the hilt," I told her as I signed the last page.

A woman came in carrying a large basket wrapped in cellophane. "Evening, Nash family. I'm Holly from parental services." She placed the basket on the table then pointed at it. "Inside this basket—which is just for the parents—you will find our card with our hotline number for you to call if you need our help. We specialize in being there as a support system for new parents. We heard this was your first child, so you might need our help in the near future."

I liked the sound of that. "Great. We will probably be giving you more than a few phone calls. We want to get this parenting thing right, don't we babe?"

Alexa nodded as she peered at the basket filled with all sorts of goodies, including a bottle of wine. "This is nice. Thank you so much." She gave the woman a smile. "And I'm sure we will be calling you guys. I have zero experience with babies, and the same goes for my hubby."

"Well, you don't hesitate to call. Not only for baby questions, which we will answer for you, but also for resources for parents and couples counseling. It's hard to transition from being a couple to being a couple who are now parents. If you're feeling anxious, angry, or sad, then give us a call. We love helping out young families."

A lot would be changing for Alexa and I in our new relationship and family. In six weeks, God willing, we'd finally be adding a completely new element to our life as a couple. Intimacy might be hard to come by with little Patty around now, but I would definitely figure out how to make time for us. Somehow.

The nurse came in just as Holly left. "Good luck to you all."

I handed the signed papers to the nurse. "Are we free to go?"

"I'll be right back with a wheelchair to take Mrs. Nash and Patty down to you. Pull the car around to the front and I'll bring them right down." She left the room then, leaving us alone.

"Wow." I ran my arms around my wife then kissed her on the lips softly. "This is it. We're taking our baby boy home."

She ran her hands around my sides as she gazed at me. "No more help. It'll just be us now. Are you ready for this?"

"Not even a little," I joked. "But we've got to do what we've got to do. I'll see you at the car, my love."

"Mi amor?" she asked as I walked away.

I stopped and turned around. "Yes?"

I saw a little hint of fear in her eyes that I'd never seen before. "We can do this, right?"

"Sure we can." *We have to. He's here. No turning back now.*

Fifteen minutes later, we were on our way home with Patty sleeping peacefully in the backseat. Alexa looked over her shoulder at him. "He's a good baby."

"He is," I agreed. And then something niggled at my soul. "Alexa, you and I need to talk."

"About what?" She gave me her full attention, running her hand along my cheek. "About how we're going to be a real man and wife? Because I am so ready for that. Even if we have to wait six weeks before we can seal the deal. Just knowing that you love me makes me feel so much better."

I took her hand, kissing it. "Me too, babe. Me too. I love you so much."

"I love you so much, too," she echoed.

"And I love Patty so much."

"Yes, me too." She sighed. "He's the best."

"And as the best, I think he deserves the best," I took a deep breath, knowing she wouldn't like what I had to say. But I thought it was what was best for our son. "I think we should consider telling the deacon and his wife about who he is to them."

Anger flashed in her dark eyes. "Are you crazy?" she shouted.

"Babe, the baby. Try not to yell," I cautioned her. "We've got fifteen more minutes in this car. If he wakes up screaming, we're in for a long fifteen minutes. And I'm not crazy. But I am feeling quite a bit of guilt over this. That man showed up out of the blue today. Don't you think that might be a sign that we're supposed to tell him about his grandson?"

"He has a grandfather," she snapped. "*My* father is Patty's grandfather. And he has a father. *You* are his father. The Soliz family has nothing to do with him."

"Yeah, but they do," I said as I tried to ignore the glare that she gave me.

"Patton, I don't want to start our family like this." She ran her hand over her forehead, as if the conversation was giving her a headache. "Patty is *your* son." She looked at me with wide eyes. "Unless you no longer want that."

"I want that," I rushed to say. "I didn't say I didn't want to be his father. I just wonder if that wasn't some act of fate, the deacon coming into our room." I wasn't sure about anything anymore. Most of all, I wasn't sure she and I would ever be able to have this conversation without her getting mad as a wet hen. "But honey, you and Patty are what matters the most in this world to me. So, if you don't want to talk about this—"

She interrupted me, "I *never* want to talk about this. You either are his father, or you are not—end of story. That family is no good. I don't care how they appear—they are no good. Our son deserves to have a good life and we can provide that for him. Without them in it."

"If that's the way you want it." It was up to her anyway. She was the biological mother, and I wasn't a biological anything. "I trust your instincts, Alexa."

"I would love it if we never spoke of this again, Patton. You've signed the birth certificate as his father, so we will never speak of things in any other way. Do you agree?"

She didn't give me much choice. "Sure, babe. I agree."

But that didn't make the guilt go away.

26

ALEXA

Sharing a bed with my husband was about to become very real. My six-week checkup with the doctor had resulted in a clean bill of health, and she'd okayed me having a sex with my husband. And boy, was I ready for that to begin.

I'd already planned ahead for the night. I felt I'd been waiting for this night for so long, so I wanted to make it special now that it was finally here. I had a bottle of Domaine Leflaive Montrachet Grand Cru chilling in the wine cooler behind the bar, plus smoked meats, cheeses, and ripe, bite-sized pieces of fruit filling a cheeseboard in the fridge.

Best of all, Patton's brother Baldwyn and his wife, Sloan had agreed to keep Patty overnight so his one-year old cousin, Audrey Rose, could get to know him better. Things were coming together rather nicely for our first night of being a real married couple.

My cell rang as I drove home. I hurried to answer the call, as Patty was fast asleep in his car seat in the back of the new car Patton had bought for me. He'd done his research and found a Genesis G90 in a warm burgundy color with supple, soft, cream-colored leather seats. I'd never ridden in, much less driven, anything so luxurious. And Patton said it was one of the safest cars on the road, too. All I knew was that I loved it. "Hey, babe."

"How'd the doctor visit go?" he asked, and I swore I could hear the smile he must've worn in his voice.

I thought I'd mess with him a bit. "Not too good."

"What?"

"Well, it looks like we'll have to wait a few more weeks before we can—well, you know." I tried not to snicker.

"A few more weeks?" came his disappointed words. For a moment, he almost sounded like a petulant teenager. I held in a laugh. "That's okay. I mean, I am disappointed and all, but your health is what really matters. Should I let Baldwyn know we don't need them to babysit tonight then?"

I didn't want him to let the babysitters go. "Okay, you got me. I was just kidding around with you. I'm good to go, the doc said. I'm heading home now to pack our son a bag for his first overnight stay with his uncle, aunt, and cousin. But I've got to tell you that I'm a little nervous about leaving him for the whole night."

"I'll keep you entertained." He chuckled. "Sloan's a great mom, so you don't have to worry. Patty will be very well taken care of. And Audrey Rose is so excited about getting to have him over, too. They're going to be great friends."

"I know they will." I had many cousins who I adored, and I wanted Patty to have that too. "I've handled the wine and appetizers. Are you going to handle dinner?"

"Dinner and dessert," he said with a slyness to his voice. "Dinner is oysters Rockefeller, artichokes, and dark chocolate-dipped figs. But the real dessert is the can of whipped cream I'm going to use on you."

My cheeks went scarlet as my entire body went up in flames. I giggled like a little girl. "Oh my gosh!"

"My gosh, indeed. You're about to find out that you have

married a skilled lover, lucky girl." Another deep chuckle told me he was kidding—but I had my bets that he was incredibly good in bed.

"Sorry, I can't bring much to the bedroom." I had no idea what I could do for him. "But I'll try my best for you."

"All you have to bring is your hot little body to our bed and let me love you like a man should love his wife."

Something crazy happened as he said those words to me. I'd never been aroused just by some simple words before, but there I was—panties damp and womanhood pulsing with what I could only assume was desire. Desire for my legal husband. No sins. Nothing bad about being with him in a sexual manner at all.

It was almost too good to be true, after all the bad things I'd been through. "You're making me hot, Patton."

"Good," his voice low, sexy, and even more arousing. "I'll see you at home in a bit then. I can't wait to get our night started. I suppose you could call it our true wedding night, Mrs. Nash."

"Yeah, I guess we could call it that." I bit my lower lip as what lay ahead of us filled my mind. "See you soon, lover." Laughter erupted as I thought about what I'd said. "That sounds silly. See you soon, mi amor."

"I can't get you alone soon enough."

"Wow," that was all I could say. I had never been so in love and so ready to experience what making love felt like. I'd had that horrible sex with the jerk, but I knew that wouldn't even come close in comparison to what Patton and I would do.

Butterflies filled my stomach as my mind ran away with me to the night ahead. As I turned the corner, I saw a red car sitting in front of the gated entrance to our home. It was parked in such a way that I couldn't go around it to get into our property.

So, I parked behind the car then got out to see who it was. "Can I help you?" I called out.

The driver's door opened and out came Alejandro Soliz. "Alejandra, I've come to talk to you about our son."

Fury flooded me and I ran at him, beating his chest with my fists. "You get the hell out of here, you son-of-a-bitch!" I'd never cussed a day in my life, but those words burst from my mouth.

He took me by the wrists to stop me from hitting him. "Alejandra, please. I came home for a visit and my father told me how he saw you and your husband in the hospital. He said the baby had come early and you'd had many problems—even almost died. I had to come see you and my son."

"He's not your son!" I shrieked at him, nearly going blind with rage. "You have no child!"

"I know you don't mean that, Alejandra."

"I was Alexa to you the last time I saw your face. Now, you're back to calling me by Alejandra? Why is that? Because you think that will make me forget all the ugly things you told me when I drove across the country to tell you that I was pregnant?" My chest was rising and falling with rapid pants. I had never felt so angry in my life.

"I will never forget those words. You told me to get rid of it—as if our baby was nothing at all. You gave up your rights that very second. Do you understand that? You gave up the right to call him yours when you said those words to me." My body shook so hard, and I finally was able to pull free from his grasp. "You are not welcome at our home. Not now—not ever. My husband and I have a son. You have nothing."

"I want to see him." He moved like lightning to get to my car then threw the back door open. "Ha! I knew he'd be in here!"

Pummeling his back with my balled-up fists, I screamed at the top of my lungs, "You get away from him!"

"Alejandra, stop. Let me look at him. He has my eyes."

I heard the sound of tires screeching to a stop then felt hands around my waist, lifting me up into the air as I flailed around, trying to get away. Then I was placed back on my feet and I saw Patton dragging Alejandro out of my car. "Get away from our son!"

Alejandro's body smashed against the gate as Patton tossed him like he was nothing more than a rag doll. He held his hands up in surrender. "Look, I'm sorry. I didn't mean to upset you."

"You came here," I pointed out. "You knew that would upset me."

"You, yes, I did expect you'd be upset with me." He jerked his head in Patton's direction. "Him, I didn't expect to encounter, quite frankly. I thought maybe you and I could talk about this without him being around. I *am* the baby's father, after all."

Patton's hands fisted at his sides. "There are so many reasons why I want to beat you until you no longer breathe. But I won't do that to you. And it's not for you that I won't kill you. It's because I *am* that boy's father, and I'm not about to go to prison for the likes of you."

"I'm sorry," Alejandro whimpered. "This was a mistake. I just wanted a chance to see my son. I didn't mean to step on anyone's toes. I didn't come here to fight. It's just that when my father told me he'd seen your baby, it hit me hard, you know? He didn't even know that he was looking at his own grandson, Alejandra. You didn't even let him know that. Me? Well, I understand that you wouldn't want me in our son's life. But my parents? You know they're good people."

For a moment, I almost felt bad. But then that feeling went away as everything he'd done and said came back to me. "They can't be that good. They did raise you. They raised you to be a liar, a cheater, and a piece of crap not worthy of having a child. I wasn't about to let your father know a thing. And I never will. You need to go and never come back. And you need to never tell your parents about this baby being yours. He's *not* yours. My husband is the legal father on all the paperwork. That is how it will stay."

Standing up tall, he asked, "And if I do tell them, then what?"

Patton stepped between us as I began growling like an animal. He put his hand on my shoulder as he looked at Alejandro. "Look, she's going to rip you apart if you don't leave. Let's put what happened between you two aside for a moment to think about who really matters here. And that's the baby boy in the backseat of that car right there. He's all that really matters here."

"Shouldn't he have the right to know who his father and his father's family are?" Alejandro asked.

"You have no right to say a thing like that, you piece of shit," I growled at him.

Patton looked back at me with wide eyes. "Babe? Did that just come out of your mouth?" Stunned, he shook his head. "Don't let him bring you down to his level. You're better than this."

Alejandro's head dropped. "He's right. You are so much better than I am. Both of you are. I'll go. I'll leave you two alone. I'm sorry I came here. I didn't mean for things to go this way at all."

"You meant to get me alone and overtake me so that you could see my baby." I knew what he'd thought would happen. "If my husband hadn't shown up, God only knows what you would've done. Isn't that right?"

"Sometimes, desperation makes us all do dumb things," he said. "I felt desperate to see my son. But like I said, I'll go."

Patton put his arm around me, pulling me close to his side. "Come on, babe. Let him leave. We're done here. He understands now that he can't be a part of our son's life. Right, Alejandro?"

Putting his hands over his face, he sounded like he was

crying. "Yeah, man. I get it. I can't be a part of his life. Now, just let me leave. Please."

"Go," I snapped. "Leave! I never want to see your face again!"

Patton held me close. "Shh. It's okay. He's leaving, babe. He gets it now."

I wasn't sure he really did. "Only God knows what I will do to you if you ever tell your parents about this baby, Alejandro Soliz."

27

PATTON

I had one feisty mamma on my hands. Alexa mumbled in Spanish under her breath, "Tonto del culo." Pacing restlessly in front of the bassinet where little Patty lay sleeping soundly, she continued her ranting. "Perdedor, debilucho, mujeriego!"

Taking her by the hand, I pulled her out of the nursery so she wouldn't wake the baby with her raving. "Come on, we don't want to wake the baby now do we?"

"He makes me so angry, Patton. You have no idea. The stupid dog!" She wasn't calming down even a little.

"Look, I get it. I get how mad you are, and you have every right to be. But you had to know he might do something like this someday." I found it hard to believe that she hadn't expected a confrontation at some point. Especially since his father had seen her in the hospital with a husband and baby. "And his father did see you with the baby."

Her eyes glistened—not with tears, but with pure hatred. "I wish that man had never laid his eyes on our child."

"You've gotta calm down." It actually made me worry about her heart. "Your heart did stop beating only six weeks ago. Take it easy. Please." I pulled her into my arms, wrapping her in my warm embrace as I rocked with her, leaning my chin on top of her head. "You've got the baby to think about now. You can't go losing your temper."

Before having the baby, I hadn't seen her ever lose her temper. I couldn't have even imagined her getting angry at someone. But it seemed like it was up and running and here to stay now. I didn't know if that was such a good thing. She could really let it fly.

"I can't help it. I felt threatened in such a horrifying way. I can't explain it." She looked up at me, her mouth set in a frown. "I can't let him take our son away from us."

"And he won't be able to do that. There's not a judge in this world who would award that man any sort of custody or even visitation. He told you to get rid of the baby, Alexa. Plus, we can afford the best lawyers in the state if he or his family even thinks about trying to take this to court." A part of me felt sorry for the guy and his family though. "But if you ever want to entertain the idea of them being part of Patty's life, you know I'll back you on whatever you want to do."

Her palms planted on my chest and she pushed me back hard. "What? You will support your son having that man in his life? You will support him having two fathers? You would do such a thing to your son, Patton?"

"You're making it sound so bad, when it's not bad at all." I wasn't sure how to talk to her about this. She was so stubborn on the matter. But it needed to be said. "You have to think about the future, baby. The fact is that our son will always be ours. But what if a day comes when he has to be told that he has a different biological father?"

"And why would that ever have to happen?" she asked as if the thought had never occurred to her.

"Let's just say that Alejandro has a daughter sometime in the near future. Let's just say that our son and Alejandro's daughter end up going to the same school. Let's just say they ended up in high school together and found an interest in each other."

"That is preposterous! You think Patty will end up falling in love with his half-sister? Ha! Ha, ha, ha." It was apparent that she thought that could never happen in a million years.

So, I brought up something a little easier for her to believe. "Okay, what about cousins then? What if he dates one of his cousins because he has no idea he's related to her?"

"That will never happen," she said sternly. "Our son won't be allowed to date until he's much older, anyways. And by then we will know if he's got any relatives in that horrible family. And we will gently persuade him not to have anything to do with any of them."

Is she even living in reality right now?

"I'm just saying that one day we might have to tell him the truth." I'd come to realize that. It was time she began to think about it, at the very least.

"Why will we have to tell him the truth, Patton? Why?" She began pacing as her hands flew around in the air. "What would that do to him if he ever finds out that you are not his natural father? I don't want to even think about it. I don't want him to ever feel bad about himself."

"Why would he feel bad about himself?" I thought that was a stretch. But then it hit me that she wasn't exactly talking about the baby. She was talking about herself. "Are you afraid that he'll think badly about you if he ever finds out that you weren't married to his biological father?"

"No," she said then stopped pacing and wrapped her arms around herself. "Well, maybe. I mean, I don't want him to think that his mother was a tramp. I want him to be able to look up to me. I want him to think of me as..."

"Hmm, as what?" I asked her. "A perfect person who has never made a questionable decision in her life? Sounds like a lot to live up to, to me. If he thinks his mother is some saint, then how will that make him feel when he makes mistakes? He needs to know that his parents are just as human as he is. He needs to know that people don't always make the right decisions in life."

"But I want him to be good. Like me." She pouted for a moment. "Like I was before that man came into my life."

"And he will be good. But he will make choices that aren't always perfect. We all do. Do you think I'm proud to admit to every woman I've ever had sex with?"

"Why?" she asked as she looked at me with worry. "Are there a lot of them?"

"Well, not a whole lot." I hadn't meant to start that conversation at all. We could save that for another day. "I just mean that I obviously made mistakes in my past, too. The same way you did. The same way Alejandro has. He's young, Alexa. Young guys do some dumb and sometimes mean things. I know I've done my fair share. Not that I'm proud of it, but I haven't always been as good as I am to you."

Her shoulders slumped and she looked as if she felt horrible. But then she stood up straight and looked me in the eyes. "Are you going to do this often?"

"Do what?" I wasn't sure what she was getting at.

"Take the side of the Soliz family," she stated.

"I'm not taking their side, honey. I'm thinking about our son." There was a difference.

"I see it as you taking their side. Because if you were thinking about our son, then you would want him to have nothing to do with those people." Her dark brows raised high as her hands moved to rest on her hips. "So, you need to think about this, Patton, and think hard. Is that boy yours or Alejandro's? You have to make up your mind. I'd rather you do it sooner than later, too. I need to know what to expect in the future. And if we have one with you or not."

The wind left my lungs. "You'd leave me over this?"

"This marriage hasn't been consummated yet," her chin jutted out stubbornly. "If we're not on the same page about our son, then I don't see the need to stay together. I won't have that family in his life. Are you with me or against me? I'll leave you to think about it." Then she turned and walked away.

Standing there breathless and lost, I watched her walk away. *What have I done?*

Five minutes rolled by before I caught my breath, and my mind began working again. I had to talk to someone who would be honest with me, not tell me only what I wanted to hear.

So, I called my older brother Baldwyn. "You on your way over with my nephew yet?" he answered my call.

"Not yet. Maybe not at all."

"You sound weird."

I felt weird. "Alexa and I just had a fight. I mean, a really bad one. And I'm not sure if she even wants to be married to me anymore."

"Good God man, what did you do?"

"I—well, I said some things maybe I shouldn't have." I hadn't seen this coming at all. "She's mad at me. Like furious."

"What the hell happened?" he asked. "She was happy as could be when she talked to Sloan earlier today."

"The Soliz kid was here when she came back from the doctor," I told him as I tried to wrack my brain as to how I was going to deal with this issue.

"Did you kick his ass? I sure hope so." Baldwyn wasn't a fighting man, so I had no idea why he'd say such a thing.

"Why would I kick his ass?"

"For so many reasons," he said. "Reason number one, he came to your home. Reason number two, he hurt the woman you love."

"I wasn't in love with her when he did that," I reminded him.

"And he came to our home because his father saw us at the hospital and told him about the baby. I'd felt sort of guilty since then. But when I told Alexa about how I felt, she got mad. Not nearly as mad as she is now, but she did get mad."

"If she got mad then, what made you think she wouldn't get mad now?" He seemed to have all the questions prepared in advance. "And what did you do or say to piss her off anyway?"

"Well, I sort of said that we had to face the fact that one day we'll have to tell Patty about his biological father and that family." I didn't see anything wrong with that, and I waited to see if my brother found anything wrong with it.

"Why would you have to tell him anything about those people?"

Crap. He thinks the same way Alexa does.

"You don't think it's important to be honest with him?" I thought he, of all people, would think honesty was the best policy.

"I'm not saying that it always has to be a secret. But while he's an impressionable kid, he doesn't need to know about them. It'll only confuse him," he said with what sounded like conviction in his voice. "Once he's older, maybe. Then that'll be something you and Alexa might think about talking to him about. Until then, it needs to be kept under wraps—for Patty's sake. No reason to go confusing the boy. It sounds like you need to keep it hush-hush for Alexa's sake too. It doesn't sound like something she's ready to parse out right now."

"But I don't think Alexa *ever* wants to tell him," I said as I started thinking that maybe I had been a little bit wrong to make a big deal out of this right now.

"The future is the future. Who knows what anyone will think by that time? He'll be grown and you two will have weathered a few storms as well. You have no idea what will happen. But for now, just be that boy's father—and only you. That guy isn't in any shape to take on the role of daddy. Not from what I've heard about him. He's a selfish jerk. You want to have him co-parenting your kid, Patton?"

"No." I hadn't thought about that. "Not at all. He's a young punk with no idea if he's coming or going. You're right. I was wrong. I should've just kept my mouth shut. I should've just had my wife's back and never brought up what went through my mind."

"Yep," he agreed. "Look, I'm your brother and I know how caring and soft-hearted you can be. Do you remember that puppy that showed up on our street when we were kids?"

"Yeah, Bones. That was what I called him." I recalled the small mixed breed well.

"Dad wanted to call the pound to pick it up, but you went running out of the house, picked it up, and brought it into our backyard. You weren't going to let anyone take that mangey mutt away from you. And you took great care of him too. You even bathed him in that mange medicine you bought with your own money from the vet's office."

"I loved that dog." It was a good memory. "And then that man came looking for his dog and knocked on our door a month later."

"And that man had that truck full of dogs in those little kennels. It was obvious that he was going to use that poor dog in some dog fighting ring," he said. "Only that wasn't obvious to you. And you were about to hand that dog over until Dad stepped in and told you to take the dog back outside to the backyard. He paid that man two hundred dollars to let you keep the dog. He knew that man wasn't going to be good to that dog at all. And Dad knew you'd never hurt it."

"Oh my god, Baldwyn. I never realized that about the guy. I thought he just loved dogs and had lots of them." I chuckled at my naiveté, but felt relieved that we'd been able to save Bones from that kind of life.

"All I'm saying is that the Soliz boy might grow up someday and be worth a shit. But he's not right now. And Patty needs good, stable parents who will nurture him and help him grow into a great man. You and Alexa can do that for Patty—all on your own. But you go mucking it up, infusing some young jerk into the mix, then who knows what might happen? Let the boy grow up, and then you can revisit this idea. What do you say?"

"I say that you're pretty damn wise, big brother. And I've got an apology to give my wife. I'll bring Patty to you soon, so I can make things right with his mother."

Good God, I've got to learn to think before I speak!

28

ALEXA

Sitting on the end of the bed, my heart pounded. I couldn't calm down. And I wasn't sure that I wanted to. If Patton was going to be feeling sorry for someone he shouldn't, then I honestly didn't see a future for us.

But I had to admit to myself that the idea of leaving him hurt me. But there was more than just me to think about now. Patty was more important.

So what if I loved Patton more than I knew was possible? So what if our marriage was just about to truly begin? All that really mattered was the well-being of the baby I'd brought into the world.

My cell phone dinged, and I took it out of my pocket to find Patton had texted me:

"I was a fool. You are right and I am wrong. And I mean that. I'm taking Patty to my brother's and I'll be back to make things up to you. So, get your fine-ass ready because your husband is about to make you his wife in every way imaginable. P.S. I left a bottle of wine and a glass next to the bedroom door so you can have some while you take a nice long bubble bath. Get ready for our second honeymoon to start,

babe. I love you to the moon and back. I'm sorry and I'm going to prove that to you very soon.

As I read his words, the anger vanished into thin air. "Oh. Okay. Good."

Since that was settled, I typed in some loving words to him to let him know that all was forgiven, and I would indeed be getting ready for our honeymoon night.

I opened the bedroom door and found the wine and the glass. Taking them with me to the tub, I poured myself a glass and then pulled my clothes off as the tub filled up with shiny, fragrant bubbles.

Nothing mattered now that we were on the same page again. We could move forward now with nothing holding us back. And I'd never wanted anything more in my life.

The long nights must've caught up to me, as I fell asleep in the tub. I woke to find Patton looking down at me. "Hey there, Mrs. Nash."

Blinking up at him, I smiled. "Hey there, Mr. Nash."

He pulled a bouquet of red roses out from behind his back. "I thought you might like these. I wanted them to remind you of how sorry I am."

"All is forgiven, mi amor." I'd never been completely naked in front of him before, and thought it was high time for something like that. So, I slowly rose up out of the bubbles. "Mind handing me a towel?"

His eyes moved up and down the length of my body. "Oh, baby. Or should I say, oh, hot mamma?"

"Let's leave Mamma out of this. Tonight, we're not parents. Tonight, we're a couple of people who have fallen head over heels in love and have just gotten married."

His nod told me he was into it. Handing me a towel, he began taking his shirt off. Each button he unhooked showed more and more of his chiseled torso.

I sucked on my lower lip, as seeing his tight abs and pecs did things to me that bordered on obscene. *I had no idea women could get hard-ons.*

Once his pants hit the floor, revealing a saluting male member that seemed to be waving at me, I began to shake. Not out of fear. Not at all. I shook because I felt such a pure, visceral need to feel him inside of me.

Scooping me up in his arms, he carried me to the bed and unceremoniously laid me down onto it. "Just so you know, there will be screaming."

"Screaming?" I asked just as he pushed my legs apart then yanked at me until my bottom was at the edge of the bed.

"Yes, lots of screaming." Kneeling in front of me, he put his hands on my knees, making chills run through me. "And hair pulling, too. Lots of hair pulling. The more you pull my hair, the more I'll do for you."

His hands grazed along my inner thighs as I sat up on my elbows to see what he was going to do. My heart raced, my mouth watered, and somewhere deep inside my body, drums began to beat.

He kept his eyes on mine as he inched forward, getting closer and closer to my newly shaved area. "Nice."

"Thanks, I thought about you when I shaved." I smiled. "I had high hopes that you meant to use the whipped cream on me in this general area."

"Later." He licked his lips. "I want to taste you and only you right now. I've hungered for you for such a long time. I don't want any other taste getting in the way."

My mouth gaped a bit as he leaned in and I watched him as he kissed me softly. "Oh, God!"

"Easy, girl," his lips grazed the spot again, making sparks fly through me. "Let's take this nice and slow."

"K." I bit my lip, unable to pull my eyes off him.

One long lick sent my head falling backward. Nothing had prepared me for this sensation. One more lick and I felt transported to another place and time. The third had me moaning with passion as I filled my hands with his hair, pulling it the way he'd said to.

His kisses went from soft to hard and wanting as he took my bottom into his hands, lifting me up as he devoured me. I cried out for mercy, but there was none. My body was wracked with an orgasm that made my toes curl under.

And then he let me go, the abrupt drop causing my bottom to bounce slightly on the bed. I looked up to see him standing over me. His cock had a large drop of white creamy stuff on the tip. He arched one brow as he looked at it then at me. "Would you like to taste me?"

I had no idea what I was doing, but I knew I needed that taste. I was like a woman possessed, moving onto my knees and taking his thick member into my hands before running my tongue over the creamy tip.. "Salty. Not bad at all." I'd had other ideas about what a man's semen tasted like. I'd been worried it would taste a little like pee, and I was relieved to find I'd been wrong.

With one discovery out of the way, I put my mouth on my man and moved it back and forth, nice and slow. Pleasing him that way did something unimaginable to me. It made me even hotter for him. It made me crazy for him. It made me feel more like a woman than I had ever felt before.

He grabbed a fistful of my hair, pulling it hard, and I loved it. Moving my mouth over him at the speed he wanted, I moaned with the sensations it gave me. If anyone had told me that this act would bring me pleasure, I would've called them a damn liar. But it did bring me pleasure. Tons of it.

I felt him get hard as a rock before he pulled me off him.

"Time to consummate this marriage. I think you're ready for me now."

He lifted me up, holding me above him and slid my body down his. My nipples were as hard as diamonds as they ran over his chest. Moving with such grace that it defied my imagination, he and I ended up on the bed with his body covering mine.

I moved my legs, spreading them for him as he eased into me. As gentle and slow as he was with me, it still burned like fire as he moved all the way into me. I screamed as the pain mixed with pleasure. "Patton!" My nails bit into his shoulders. "Yes!"

His mouth moved along my neck, licking, nibbling, peppering my flesh with hot kisses that took my mind away from the searing pain that eventually turned into something exactly the opposite of that.

Arching my body, I wanted to meet each thrust he made. I wanted more of him inside of me. I wanted to feel him deep—as deep as he could possibly get.

"I don't want this to end," I moaned.

He flipped over onto his back then pulled me to sit up on top of him. "Then it won't. We can go all night."

Moving as if I was riding a horse, I laughed at how free I felt with him. "All night long?"

"All night long." He grabbed my wrists and pulled them above his head, positioning me so he could take a nipple into his mouth, sucking gently on it.

My breasts began to fill right away with milk, but the way it felt was vastly different from when my baby fed from them. Perhaps because my baby didn't use his tongue to entice me the way his father did. The light licks across my hard nipple made me tingle all over.

"Looks like you won't be hungry for dinner for some time," I joked with him.

He pulled his mouth off me just long enough to say, "I'm only hungry for you, wife." His hands moved around my back, pushing me to him as his tongue ran between my breasts as he sat up.

Rocking with him, I moved my legs to wrap around him as we both sat up. Skin to skin, our perspiration mixing; the smell of sex hung in the air. It intoxicated me until I couldn't even think anymore.

We rolled all over that king-sized bed until we couldn't breathe. Both of us satisfied, both of us panting, both of us smiling. I knew then that this was what making love was all about. It was about sharing yourself with one another, and not having to think about a thing. It was about doing what came naturally. Leaving embarrassment at the door and doing whatever we wanted without worry.

Love made everything different. And I thought that was as it should me. "I love you more than you will ever understand, mi amor." Caressing his handsome face, I saw my future in his blue eyes.

"Our love will never stop growing, my sweet, sexy wife. I will be everything you need me to be for you and our family." He kissed the top of my nose then sighed. "You are the epitome of love. Wholesome, kind, giving, caring– and you're hot, too."

Laughing, I loved how he made his little jokes. "When I married you that day in front of that fat Elvis impersonator, I couldn't help but wish that we were getting married in the church we both grew up in. But now, I'm glad we did it our way. Our love is different. It's a little funny, a little sexy, and a little on the old-fashioned side."

"I like it just the way it is." He pulled me to lie on top of him. "I think we're going to have a great life together, Mrs. Nash."

"Unless we starve to death first." I jumped up and ran out of the room, then came back with the oysters I found in the fridge and two ice-cold beers. "Our bodies need replenishment. I think alcohol and aphrodisiacs will do the trick."

Sitting up, he took the tray from me, putting it on the bed. "Take a seat and let me introduce you to a yummy treat." He knew I hadn't eaten oysters or anything like them before. Picking one up, he put the shell against his lower lip then let the rather disgusting grey slimy thing inside slide into his mouth. He kept his mouth open to show me how it slid right down his throat without him chewing it at all. Then he took a swig of the beer. "Ah," he said, making it sound refreshing. "You try."

"Oh, I don't know." I looked at the gelatinous goo on the jagged oyster shell. "The green stuff and the yellow stuff on top don't make it look any better."

"The green stuff is spinach." He picked up another one. "And the yellow stuff is hollandaise sauce. I know you'll like it if you try it."

I'd brought it to our bedroom instead of the other goodies for a reason. I wanted to try new things. He'd eaten one and he made it look sort of good. But not completely. "So, I can trust you, right?"

He nodded. "The oyster is tasteless. It's the other foods that you'll taste. And as long as you don't try to chew it, you'll like it."

"Just put it to my lips, let it slide down my throat, and that's it." I took the shell out of his hand and put it to my lips. "How does that old saying go? Through the lips and over the tongue, look out tummy because here it comes?"

"Sounds right to me." He grinned at me. "I'll give you a nice long kiss after you eat it."

Slurp. "Ah," I said then took a drink of the beer. "I'll take that kiss now."

Leaning over the large round tray, I met him in the middle and our lips met. His tongue slipped through my lips then played with mine and I played right back.

When he ended his kiss, I sighed as he said, "This is it. This is the life. I have found what I wasn't even looking for. And I've found it with probably the one woman on this planet that I never thought I'd find it with."

He chuckled and shook his head. "I feel like an idiot for not realizing it sooner. But you were untouchable. You were taboo. And now you and I are husband and wife, and your entire family is happy about it. Even your brother. Ha! I wouldn't have believed this if anyone had told me. Would you?"

I had to agree. "Patton, this is fate, that's what it is. A miracle. And like most miracles, as my mother says, we are not to think too much about them. God's gifts are often things we never see coming. I never saw this coming and neither did you." I had to laugh. "What you must've thought when my brother came to you, asking you to marry his pregnant little sister."

He took another oyster, gulping it down then chasing it with some beer. "I thought, 'Huh? What?' But then I thought about you being so afraid, not knowing what to do, or who to turn to, where to go. I knew then that I had to make things easy for you."

"And you did." I leaned over, kissing him on the cheek. Then I ate another oyster. "You know, these aren't half bad."

"Right?" He ate another. "And they make you randy, baby."

"Randy?" I had no idea what he was talking about.

"Yeah." He handed me one more. "I'll let you tell me how they make you feel."

I ate the third oyster and felt nothing. "I have no idea what you're talking about with this randy nonsense."

Before I knew it, we'd finished the entire tray. I picked it up and put it on the dresser then turned to find Patton spread out on the bed. He held one rose out of the bouquet he'd given me as an apology for our argument. "I'd like to run these soft petals all over your body."

Moving across the room, I found his smile cheeky. I loved

this roguish side of him. "Mmm, now why does that sound like such a great idea?"

"Are you kidding me right now?" He moved over me as I lay on the bed. Barely touching me with the soft rose, he whispered in my ear. "You said it yourself, the oysters are aphrodisiacs."

"Doesn't that mean they're appetizers? Like a fancy word for them?" I had honestly thought that's what it meant.

"Randy means horny. Or aroused is probably a nicer word for it." His lips moved over my skin, barely touching, the same as he did with the rose. "And aphrodisiacs are foods that make you randy." I could feel his smile on my skin.

The flower moved over my breasts, then down the middle of my stomach before being whisked across my womanhood. I suddenly realized why my body arched and I moaned in ecstasy. "Oh, *randy*." I closed my eyes, falling into the abyss of bliss as he kissed every last inch of my body. "Yeah, I get it now. I do feel aroused. But randy is a much better word for it. At least I can tell you when I feel aroused without everyone knowing what I'm saying."

"Sure, baby." His lips moved to find mine. "No one will ever know what you're talking about if you say that." He laughed, and his freely given happiness sent me over the edge again.

EPILOGUE
PATTON

One year later...

Patty and Audrey Rose ran along the path in front of us at the zoo. "El-e-phant," Audrey sounded out as they stopped in front of the elephant exhibit to stare in wonder at the huge creatures. At only two, my niece was already a chatty girl, thanks to her mother's diligent work.

Patty pointed at the animal nearest to him. "Big!"

Alexa clapped and laughed, just as she did every time our son used a real word. It brought her more joy than just about anything. "Yes, Patty. That is a *big* elephant. Great job, buddy."

"Boys mature slower than girls do," I thought I would remind my wife. "It's not likely that we'll be hearing full sentences out of Patty when he turns two."

"Nonsense." Her hands went right to her hips. "Boys can learn just as fast as girls can. It's the teacher that makes the difference. And I've been learning from Sloan, so our son is going to have an awesome teacher in me."

I could see there would be no arguing with her over this. "I'm sure you'll achieve your goal then."

"I'm sure I will." She was probably right, too. When that woman put her mind to something it usually came to fruition.

Audrey Rose took Patty by the hand, pulling him along with her as they ran to the next exhibit. "Look at the monkeys, Patty!" she squealed with delight. "Love monkeys!"

They skidded to a stop in front of the cage and the monkeys went wild, making all sorts of noise. Patty covered his ears. "Loud."

Alexa couldn't believe it. He'd never said that word before. "Yes, Patty!" She ran to him, picked him up, and swirled him around as she kissed his chubby cheek. "They are loud. You are Mamma's smart little boy, aren't you?" She gazed at him with so much love in her dark eyes that it made me the slightest bit envious.

"Smart," Patty said, delighting his mother even more.

"Oh, my goodness! Patty, Momma's so proud of you." She put him down as Audrey Rose tugged at her shirttail. "Yes?"

Audrey Rose pointed at her chest. "Smart too, Auntie."

Laughing, Alexa picked up her niece and swung her around, making giggles erupt out of her. "Of course, you are smart too, you little wonder child. And Auntie and Unckie love you very much."

I saw a gleam flicker in my wife's eyes as she looked at me and set the girl back on her feet. Audrey Rose grabbed Patty's hand and off they went to see the tigers. "Tigers! Come on, Patty."

Alexa sauntered up to me, looped her arm through mine, then leaned her head on my shoulder. "How long should we wait?"

I had no idea what she was talking about. "For what?"

"No longer than a year," she said. "Maybe we shouldn't wait at all."

I began to get what she was drifting toward. "Your body might not be ready for that."

"I've been taking lots of vitamins." She ran her hand up and down my arm seductively. "I have a checkup with Doctor Barclay in a few weeks. She could tell me if things look good, right?"

"Patty isn't even out of diapers yet." I wasn't too keen on having two kids who were still in diapers. "What if we have another baby *after* he's out of diapers?"

"What if we don't?" she asked with a grin then kissed my cheek. "What if we have a little girl this time? What if she has long dark hair that I can brush and style and braid? And what if she has your gorgeous blue eyes?"

"I'd say she'd be a real beauty," I said jokingly. "But honey, really, I think you're asking too much of your body too soon. Patty just turned one a couple of months ago. If you got pregnant now, he wouldn't even been two when the new baby is born."

"He'd turn two soon after." She huffed then pulled away from me, her hands going to her hips again. "Do you think I can't handle a newborn and a toddler? Just tell me if you think that."

I'd learned to pick and choose my battles with my feisty wife. And this wasn't a battle I would be picking. "Come here, little mamma." I grabbed her hand, pulling her back to my side and running my arm around her waist. "If you get the okay from the doctor, then I'm all for it."

"Really?" She smiled as she looked into my eyes. "Because I want you to want this as much as I do."

"Why do I get the feeling that you've been thinking about this for awhile and this is just the first I'm hearing of it?"

"It came to me last week, to be honest. But I thought you

would say pretty much what you have said. So, I didn't say anything then, but I did make the phone call to the doctor's office to set up an appointment for a checkup. That way I could get the all-clear from the doctor before I spoke to you about this." She looked at the kids, who ran back and forth in front of the tiger's cage, mimicking its movements. "I really want to try for a little girl, Patton."

"And if we have another boy, then what?" I thought she needed to know that could happen.

"Well, I guess we'll just have to try again in a couple of years. You're a great father and you make having babies easy." As far as compliments went, that was a pretty awesome one.

Kissing her on the top of her head, I hugged her. "You're a great mother, and you make having babies pretty easy too. But you should know that I'm not quite past that heart-stopping incident. That really scared me, baby. What if that happens again?"

"It was from the drug, Patton." She smacked me in the arm. "My heart is fine. You know that."

She had no idea how much that had affected me. "I still have nightmares about that, Alexa. I can't recall a time I've been more afraid in my life."

"I'm not going anywhere, mi amor. If the doctor shares your concerns, then I will follow her orders. You know she wouldn't put my life at risk. We can trust her judgment."

I knew I had to get over my fear of losing her. And what better way to get rid of a fear than facing it. "Oh, hell. I'm in, babe. Let's have a baby."

She held up one finger. "Only if Doctor Barclay says that I'm healthy enough for that."

This woman always has to get in the last word.

∽

Alexa

A month had passed since I'd gone to see my doctor and gotten the news that I could have another baby if I wanted. But so far, no matter how hard we tried, nothing was happening.

And we'd tried—hard. Not that I was complaining about that part of it.

"A solid month, Patton. That's how long it's been. We have sex three times a day, every day, and still nothing." It was hard not to blame myself. "Maybe my womb isn't any good and I just got lucky the first time."

He sat down on the bed beside me, running his hand through my bed-styled hair. He placed the pink stick with a minus sign on the bedside table beside. I'd taken a pregnancy test each morning for the last month. "It's only been a month, baby. There's nothing wrong with your womb. Your patience? Well, there might be something wrong with that."

I punched him in the arm. "Stop trying to make me laugh. This is serious. I got pregnant with Patty after only a few times. So why is it taking longer this time?"

"Maybe we're going about this the wrong way." He got up and went to get something out of one of the dresser drawers. Coming back, I saw the calendar in his hand. "How about we don't go at it like rabbits for a while. Let's wait a week without having sex. I'll let my sperm build up and then we'll go for it. Sounds like a good plan to me. What do you think?"

"I think you might be right. We're using it all up." I took the calendar from him then got up and found a pen to mark one week from that day. "So, next Saturday it is." I tapped the pen on my chin. "Do you think morning, noon, or night would be better?"

"Night," he said quickly. "We'll make a date out of it. I'll take you out for a nice dinner, then maybe some dancing, and then we'll come home and make a baby."

I wanted it so bad that it hurt. Running my hands over my flat stomach, I looked at myself in the mirror over the dresser. "I just want to see a nice round belly again."

Patton came up behind me, running his arms around me and placing his hands on mine. "We *will* make this happen. Trust me, honey. I'll give you what you want. I always do."

When the weekend rolled around, I felt butterflies in my stomach as we dropped Patty off with his aunt and uncle. I had no idea why I felt so nervous about going out with my husband and the rest of the night we had in store, but I had a crazy amount of anxiety.

When he came to get back into the car, I blurted out a decision I'd just made. "I don't want to have a baby anymore."

"Wait." He looked at me with narrowed eyes as if he couldn't believe what I'd just said. "What? You don't want to have a baby now?"

"It's too much pressure." I held up my hand to show him how it shook. "My heart is pounding. My nerves are shot. It's crazy. I can't do it."

"Then we won't do it, honey. No big deal at all. There's absolutely no reason for you to feel pressure about having a baby." He put the car in drive. "We'll just go out for a nice dinner then head home where we can go to sleep or do whatever. It'll be fine. Just relax. You've been on pins and needles for a month about this."

"I'm sorry." I knew I was the one who was at fault here. "You're right. I have been on pins and needles. I think I just want to give you a child of your own so badly that it's making me sort of crazy."

"I've got a child of my own. Patty is my son." He looked at me out of the corner of his eye. "If that's why you really wanted to have another baby, then that's not a good reason."

"You really feel that way about him, Patton?" I'd had my little worries about him not feeling like he was really Patty's father—I didn't realize how much it had been weighing on me until that moment.

"I do." He looked at me straight in the eyes as he pulled to the side of the road. "I was there with you through the whole pregnancy. I was there when he was born. And I've been there every day, every night, through the feedings every two hours. That boy is my son. And no one had better ever say anything different."

Finally, I relaxed and smiled at my husband, the love of my life. "Of course. You make me so happy, mi amor."

"You make me happy too." He took my hand, kissing it softly. "You know something, babe?"

"What?" I couldn't stop looking at my gorgeous husband with his sparkling eyes.

"I think we'll find our happily ever after whether we have more children or not. I love you. My life is with you. And that's all that really matters."

"I feel the same way."

And with that, we went on our date as planned. No pressure. No worries. No fears that my husband felt short-changed in any way by our son not being his biological child.

One month later, I was cleaning the bathroom that my husband and I shared. Pulling open the cabinet door to clean underneath the sink, I noticed an unopened box of feminine products. Products that I should've used by now.

Turning around, I ran to the medicine cabinet to see if I had any pregnancy tests left and found only one sitting there on the shelf. A few minutes later, I ran through the house, waving the pink stick with a plus sign as I went. "Patton! Mi amor! We're pregnant! We're going to have another baby!"

And now we will live happily ever after.

The End

www.ingramcontent.com/pod-product-compliance
Lightning Source LLC
LaVergne TN
LVHW021712060526
838200LV00050B/2618